D1234607

LOST IN SPACE: Promised Land

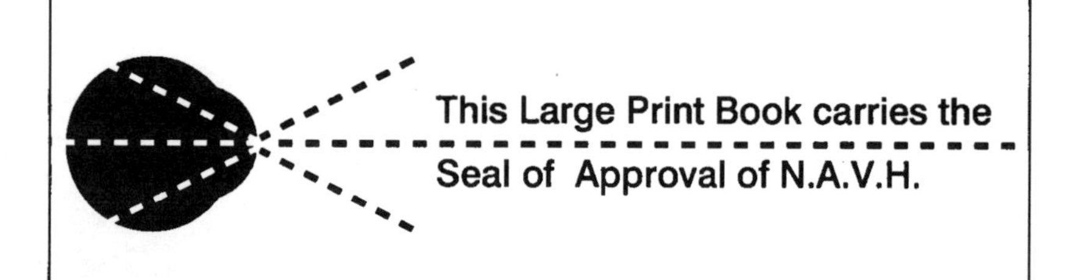
This Large Print Book carries the
Seal of Approval of N.A.V.H.

LOST IN SPACE: Promised Land

PAT CADIGAN

G.K. Hall & Co. • Thorndike, Maine

Published in 1999 by arrangement with
HarperCollins Publishers, Inc.

G.K. Hall Large Print Science Fiction Series.

The text of this Large Print edition is unabridged.
Other aspects of the book may vary from the original edition.

Set in 16 pt. Plantin.

Printed in the United States on permanent paper.

Library of Congress Cataloging in Publication Data

Cadigan, Pat, 1953–
Lost in space : promised land / Pat Cadigan.
p. (large print) cm.
ISBN 0-7838-8675-6 (lg. print : hc : alk. paper)
1. Large type books. I. Title.
[PS3553.A3135L67 1999]
813′.54—dc21 99-15812

For Carnival Diablo
December 1993
Scott McClelland
Julianne Manchur
Ryan Madden
Commemorating our own strange trip
through time and space

Chapter One

I'm looking at a former fighter pilot.

The thought was in Don West's head before he could suppress it. He kept staring his reflection in the eye as he dried off from the brief but welcome shower.

Former fighter pilot Don West . . .

Don West, formerly a fighter pilot . . .

His reflection looked tired. No, not *tired,* exactly. Faded. It was a look he'd seen on pilots who had been grounded before their time by spinal injuries, eye hemorrhages, vertigo — things that went from acute to chronic and put paid to your working life. If you had enough years of service, they mustered you out on a fat retirement/disability package and let you come to the annual banquet. If you didn't, they made you an instructor at the academy and *forced* you to come to the annual banquet.

He and Jeb never could decide which would be worse. Maybe because when you were born to fly, being grounded was just another way of saying buried, and there wasn't anything worse than that. So the idea of there being a *worst* way to be grounded wasn't the point.

But now, West thought, he might well have come up with something that really did qualify for worst of the worst: still able, but not a chance. If Jeb could see him now.

Unless he got a *real* wild hair and decided to take this overgrown family camper on a joyride — give old John and Maureen a scare, roust them out of their resignation. Assuming anything could do that now. Will would be entertained, Penny would be Penny, and with any luck it would scare that ratbag Smith into a coronary.

Of course, Judy would just bring him back. Hippocratic oath: I hereby swear to resuscitate everyone, even the illegitimate offspring of the mating of a slug with a weasel.

That would make Smith a sleazel, Don thought, and laughed. Good one. Too bad there wasn't a buddy on hand to share it with.

He realized he'd been standing in the small shower-room staring into the mirror over the sink for something like five minutes. Better get a move on. Not that there would be anyone lining up to use the shower; the next one wasn't scheduled till tomorrow, when Judy's ration would be distilled. So clever of Maureen Robinson to figure out exactly how much water each person on board would need for the sake of cleanliness and then dole it out in weekly measures. So clever of them all to number exactly seven, though he wasn't crazy about giving Smith an equal ration along with the rest of them. The *sleazel* was an interloper, an intruder, had tried to *kill* them for God's sake. But he still got an equal share of the water, not to mention the food.

Let it go, he told himself firmly. *Let it go and more it on out.* He began dressing quickly, remembering that Judy had seen him heading toward the shower and she would know how long he'd been. She just couldn't resist teasing him about how long he took in the bathroom. *Men who say women take a long time in there obviously never had to share one with you, Major. Still finding a lot to admire, are we?*

The first time it had been mildly clever. The second time, more mild, less clever. The eighth time, more than mildly boring, and the sixteenth time, excruciating. Sometime after that he'd lost count, but it had passed through boring to annoying to maddening, and was now approaching the limits of justifiable homicide.

And that was just another day on the *Jupiter Two*, folks, whatever day that might happen to be. He sighed and opened the door a crack just so he could make sure Judy wasn't out there waiting for him.

She wasn't, but Penny was.

The moodiest Robinson of them all, possibly even more dangerous than Zachary Ratbag Smith, she was, as usual, wearing her patented Pubescent Pout, a psycho scowl that was supposed to serve, by turns, as a sultry come-hither look, a no-trespassing sign, or the portent of an imminent tantrum. The only thing that frightened him more than one of her tantrums was when her hormones reactivated her crush on him. Worse, however, was the fact that he couldn't seem to tell the difference between one state of mind and another. Adolescence *and* lost in space — he'd have been sympathetic if he hadn't been trapped in the same spacecraft with her.

Don closed the door and rested his forehead against it. How was it that every time you thought things couldn't get worse, they did?

Glaring at the bathroom door with murder in her heart, Penny thought, *I'd give you a credit card and tell you to go buy a clue, Major God's-Gift-to-Females, but we all know there's no place to shop.*

In the hallway, a careful distance from the bathroom door, she shifted from one foot to the other. Surely he hadn't forgotten — *again* — that all the other bathroom facilities had been shut down and there was now only *one* toilet?

She gathered her willpower and glared at the closed bathroom door, imagining that all her anger was concentrated into rays shooting out of her eyes. *You* will *remember the other toilet is shut down, you* will *come out of there. You will come out* now. *Now. Now. Now. Nownownownownow-nownownownow*—

Miraculously, the door opened a crack. Penny wasn't sure whether to be scared or delighted. Half a second later, it slammed shut again and she groaned aloud. This was *unbearable.* This was *torture.* Even *real* prisoners of war got to go to the bathroom.

Well, that was grown-ups for you — the most

unfair, selfish, and insensitive creatures in God's creation. They thought they were entitled to anything and everything any time of the day or night, just by virtue of their *age,* just because they'd managed to *last longer* than anyone else. For crying out loud! And it didn't matter what it was, either. If a kid wanted or needed it, and grown-ups could take it away or spoil it somehow, they made sure they did.

Her father was as bad as any of them, equal to Superpilot in there. She'd wanted to sit quietly on the bridge, dictating a new cycle of poems into her journal, *Star Songs of the Dream Dancer,* but Daddy Big-Brain had chased her out, complaining he couldn't *think* with her chatter-chatter-chatter.

Like *he* had anything to think about. They were lost, right? Completely, utterly, totally *lost,* and their best hope was to find someplace to set down where there was some breathable air, fresh water, and edibles, and no weird time-quakes to tear it all apart.

So, all you had to do was turn on the navigational unit, right? Right. Wake me when it's Earth-type and toast me a bagel, light, plenty of cream cheese, no kippers, thanks a lot.

But *nooooooooo.* Dr. Big-Head John Robinson, the Great Brain who had gotten them all into this mess, he had to *think.* She should have reminded him what had happened the last time he'd done the old *thinking* thing. But then, being a grown-up, it wouldn't have occurred to him that there was nothing to do around here if you were still alive except breathe, wait to eat, sleep, and try not to die of boredom.

She'd been tempted to scream all that at him in one long, loud breath. Just blow right up in his face and let him *think* about *that.* Instead, she had just glowered at him and slipped off to try to find some other place with a view of the stars. But the *Jupiter Two*, which had looked as enormous as a cathedral in the beginning, seemed to have shrunk to the size of a closet over the months they had been trapped in it. Suddenly, there was nowhere she could go without running into someone else. Well, nowhere but her room, but if she had to spend any more waking hours than necessary in that — that *capsule,* she really would explode. She'd have a screaming fit, she'd — she'd —

She marched up to the bathroom door. "Dammitall, Don West!" she hollered, bashing the call button with her fist. "There are *other* life-forms on this blasted spaceship besides you *and they all have bladders!*"

By God, that girl is *a genius.*

Lying on the narrow bed in his quarters, Dr. Zachary Smith folded one arm behind his head and gazed up at the eyedropper he was holding in his other hand. The half-milliliter of clear liquid it contained looked purer and cleaner than water, and he was sure that this wasn't just an illusion born of wishful thinking combined with the side effects of what he called the Kiss of Bliss.

His hand was quite steady, in spite of the fact that Penny's agonized cry was echoing musically in his brain. Another indication that the Kiss was therapeutic under the circumstances, which anyone would have to admit were far more extreme than the relatively normal stress of med school. Med school was where he had first become acquainted with this enchanting substance.

His classmates had had much more of an appreciation for it than he'd had at the time. The politest name he could remember for it back in those days had been Head Job, which had made it sound far less appetizing than it actually was, at least to him.

Not that he'd ever been much for informally experimenting with drugs. *Experimenting?* In that context, the word was a joke. As if there was something constructive about slurping or snorting or injecting odd combinations of chemicals so you could get completely wrecked.

At least you had to have some intelligence for the Kiss. You had to know flow to distill it from some rather common and unexciting prescription remedies, how to heat it to exactly the right temperature for precisely fifteen seconds. After it cooled, half a milliliter was enough to send you into a better world for eight hours and the come-down afterwards was actually bearable. No hangover, no unpleasant side effects, no brain damage, no problem. Except for the fact that it didn't take too many doses before you were addicted.

Even so, the addiction wasn't all that bad, no worse than tobacco, proscribed for generations but still traded on better black markets everywhere. Or it had been, anyway, at the time he had unwittingly and unwillingly left Earth. Tobacco — now *that* was a stupid drug. Shown to cause some of the worst and most disfiguring forms of cancer in humans, expensive, and guaranteed to send you to an agonizing death, and some people still couldn't get enough of it.

Whereas the Kiss would at least stimulate your brain, especially your imagination. It would take you on a gentle journey and afterwards leave you feeling refreshed, not half-killed with toxins and carcinogens. Addiction seemed a small price to pay for the Kiss. More like a privilege, actually, or so the dealers used to say when they were trying to sell you the stuff.

Most people bought rather than distilling their own, the way he had the few times he'd wanted to try it. Back then, he had found the experience interesting though not compelling. After indulging three times, he had filed the whole thing away under Could Be Useful Later, along with some recently acquired information about the Dean of Life Sciences, which he'd been sure the woman would pay to keep hushed. He'd been right about both.

Funny though — he couldn't remember any

more what the Dean's expensive (for her) secret had been. The formula for the Kiss of Bliss, on the other hand, had stuck with him unfailingly. As if he and it had combined to form a new molecule, he thought and smiled. Would that he could combine with it to become a new form of life and somehow escape this overdone mobile home in reality, and not just in his Kissed dreams.

A picture congealed in his inebriated brain: the Robinson clan as classic Okies from several generations in the past. Maw and Paw, the young'uns, and the hired hand, all their belongings packed in a truck as they fled the ecological disaster that had turned arable land into dust that blew away in the wind.

Oh yes, *very* classic image, terribly fitting. He could see them all in cheap, tattered cotton clothing, barefoot, wide-eyed, thinking they were headed for the promised land. Planets whose streets were paved with gold, where money grew on trees, and champagne flowed like water. Uh-*huh*.

And when they arrived in the interstellar equivalent of the Okies' promised land, what then? Would the Robinson clan be herded into campgrounds with the rest of the universe's illiterate refugees?

He could picture it. There they'd be, just one more group of undereducated, underprepared nomads who had no place among the higher orders of life that *really* ran the universe. Would they be held in — what had those places been called? Hoovervilles, that was it. (Smith frowned; the damnedest things would surface in your memory when you were stoned.)

Interstellar migrants in a camp awaiting placement, the high and mighty Robinsons and their high and mighty hired hand would get their comeuppance. They'd discover that their would-be giant intellects were as ants' next to the real titans of the universe, beings so advanced that they were, frankly, gods.

And what would the gods of the universe do with the puny Robinsons? Make them house servants? Bathroom attendants? Or just all-purpose, general-use, unskilled manual-labor slaves?

In his mind's eye, the image of the old Hoovervilles began to morph into an entirely different sort of camp, the kind that gave pause even to a cold-blooded bastard like himself. As the girl-genius Penny herself would have put it, *Don't go there.*

He put the dropper under his tongue and squeezed the bulb hard, feeling the Kiss pour over the tender sublingual tissue. Moments later, the horrible images were fading from his mind as the Kiss spread through him.

Well, *that* was better. Talk about the damnedest things surfacing in your mind when you were stoned. You had to be real careful what thoughts you let enter your head when you were trapped alone and friendless in the depths of space, with no return date in sight.

Maybe he could convince the gods of the universe that he wasn't actually *with* the Robinsons . . .

On the level below the bridge, the youngest member of the *Jupiter Two* crew sat facing an oddly shaped robot that looked like the metal mutation of a crab crossed with a scorpion.

"Can you feel any difference?" Will asked the robot.

"I have no capacity for feeling, *Will Robinson,"* said the robot.

Will squeezed his eyes shut and tried to count to ten. He made it to four. "Okay. Can you tell there's something different about you?" he asked through gritted teeth.

"Where would this difference show itself?"

"In your head." Will took a breath. "I mean, your brain. Your neutral network. I changed the arrangement so you're getting more parallel processing without an increase in the actual number of processors. Do you feel more — I mean, do you sense anything different about your, uh, senses? How information comes through your interface?" he added quickly, hoping it was the right way to state the question. Computer intelligence was capable of just about anything but it always came down to basic programming — unless you knew, or could figure out, the correct way to state the command, you were crippled. Boy, computer intelligence was *stupid."*

"What would be the basis for comparison?" the robot asked in its impassive voice. *Supposedly* impassive. Lately, Will thought he was detecting a hint of mockery to it. If that wasn't his imagination, then he had made his breakthrough and brought the artificial intelligence to consciousness. In which case, the bad news was, the consciousness had Penny's disposition and he'd end up taking it apart with a hammer.

"Repeat: what would be the basis for comparison?" said the robot.

"Didn't you record your previous experiences before I made the change?" Will asked it impatiently.

"Unknown. There is no record."

"Then you didn't." Will sighed. "Why didn't you save any of your files before I altered you?"

"All files were present."

"Yes, but —" Will had to force himself not to pound on the robot with both fists. "You just said there was no record of any files from before I altered you."

"There is no record of previous perceptions."

"Okay, okay, okay." Will nodded, trying to think. "Can you record your perceptions of your interface *now?*"

The head module rose slightly. Will heard the unmistakable sound of processors overclocking to overload in a remarkably short time.

"No," said the robot, and died for the fifth time in as many hours.

Maureen Robinson lifted her head at the sound of Will shouting at the robot. In other circumstances, she might have gone out to him from the refuge of the room she was sharing (though not at this very moment) with John. But she knew if she did, she'd just start shouting herself. Will would return the favor, and they would end up shouting at each other until someone — John or Judy, most likely, since Don West and Penny knew better — came to pull them away from each other's throats. Which would be the signal for them both to turn on the intervening party and rip him, or her, or them, to shreds. Figuratively speaking, of course.

Thank God for that "of course." But how long before something of a physically violent nature does *happen? What do we do after someone finally raises a hand in anger against one of the others, what then?*

She thought of a very old poster reproduction she had seen in an exhibit on twentieth-century popular culture at the Museum of Modern Art. Two cartoon vultures perched high on a desert scene; one turns to the other and says something like, "The hell with waiting, I'm gonna kill something."

That about summed it up as far as Maureen Robinson was concerned. That captured the threshold they were all approaching perfectly, far better than any high-flown psychiatric description of the effects of cabin fever on the human organism. She doubted that even the most accomplished clinician could capture the torture of waiting for *if* to tune into *when.*

She hadn't talked any of this over with John. Aside from the fact that she wasn't actually speaking to him right now (or for the foreseeable future, if she could help it), it wouldn't help navigate or replenish any of their dwindling supplies, and so he wouldn't want to hear it. He had made that very plain the last time she had spoken to him.

If it doesn't pertain to us finding our way back to Earth, discovering a source of energy or food, or averting an imminent disaster such as a hull breach or becoming one with a neutron star, then it comes under the general heading of complaints, he had said in that infuriatingly lofty tone he had developed for press conferences back in Houston. *Complaints are handled by the Complaint Department, if anyone ever opens one. I can guarantee you right now that it* won't *be me.*

The John Robinson School of Rhetoric — never hesitate to use a hundred words where two will do.

And how about the Maureen Robinson School of Coping? asked a little voice in her mind. The voice of reason, no doubt. *How does that one go? Never hesitate to let someone annoy you, even when he isn't around?*

Yeah, that was the voice of reason, all right. Had to be. Either that or the voice announcing her definite arrival in funny-farm land. Which begged the question: Out here, was there *really* a difference?

She rolled back into the middle of the queen-sized bed and spread out her arms and legs to remind herself how much she enjoyed stretching out alone. Small pleasures; concentrate on the small pleasures, they would keep you from going mad long enough to pull yourself together.

Something in the air changed; she could smell it. Sitting up, she saw John standing in the doorway gazing at her in that half soulful, half measuring way he'd acquired over the last however-many-hundred hours they'd been out here in the Big Nowhere. Actually, he'd probably always had that look and she'd just been too hypnotized to see it the way it really was. She'd probably mistaken it for *depth* or something, an indicator of the noble poet-scientist he'd convinced himself that he actually was.

She could feel her own face settle into stony, unwelcoming lines of hostility. Just so he'd know that whatever great pronouncement he was going to make now wasn't going to cut any ice with her. *If it doesn't pertain to us finding our way back to Earth, discovering a source of energy or food, or averting an imminent disaster such as a hull breach or getting sucked into a neutron star, go suck an egg. Got that?*

Maddeningly, he said nothing, only kept looking at her. She glared lack, defiant, even as her resolve started to melt. *You're just playing right into the pattern, it's just cabin fever and nothing else. If no one else can keep their heads straight, then it's doubly important that* you *stay sane, just because you* can. *Even if it* is *a pain in the ass.*

"What is it?" she said at last, trying to soften her tone.

His eyes narrowed warily but he still didn't speak. His face was like a mask now and she realized that she actually couldn't read him at all. She didn't know whether he was happy, sad, enraged, thoughtful, afraid, physically ill, or completely numb. He might have just done anything; he might be about to do anything. She couldn't tell. In over a quarter of a century of marriage, she couldn't remember ever being unable to read John Robinson; the realization was a cold sinking in her chest.

"John," she said firmly, keeping her voice as even and neutral as possible. "Is there something wro— something you want to tell me?"

Oh, God — Were his eyes welling up? Was he about to *cry?* If John broke down, if he was unable to function, it would fall to her and that testosterone-soaked flyboy in leather pants to run things together, and she wasn't sure she could go fifteen seconds in that muscle-head's company, not the way things were right now —

"Maureen," he said, his voice low and only a little shaky, "I need you to come and look at something. I need to know."

"What do you need to know?"

"I need to know if what I'm seeing is really there." He straightened up, unconsciously standing at attention before her, his eyes resolutely dry. "And if it isn't there, I need to know if we had the foresight to stock antipsychotics. Because I'll have to take some."

Judy came out of the trance she had fallen into in front of the monitor on her desktop. The fractal mandala she had been contemplating as an exercise in meditation shifted unnoticed. Voices — sounded like her parents. They weren't going to fight again, were they? She thought she'd managed to put a lid on that by threatening them both with a coma cocktail in their ersatz coffee if they couldn't control their bitchiness. That word actually described her father's disposition better than her mother's. Maureen Robinson's iron-willed self-mastery came out as a cool that went all too icy and, you should pardon the expression, frigid, and practically never went too far in the direction of warmth.

Well, if they were going to go for each other's throats after all, she'd just have to go to Plan B. The hypos were ready, correct dosages in each one. Pink syringe for Dad, blue for Mom — her own private joke. Don West's syringe was also pink. If she had to shoot him up, she would be sure to let him see it before his eyes rolled up in his head. Insult to injury, perhaps, but if it reached the point where she really did have to shoot him up, he would definitely have it coming. Smith's syringe was a poisonous green, with a double dose.

Penny and Will, on the other hand, could be taken care of by skin patches. A quick slap on the neck and the babies would sleep the night through, the night in question being the dark night of their souls. But *only* in case of an emergency; only then, and for no other reason. No matter how much any of them got under her skin — or up her nose, as Smith put it (what a way that man had with words) — no matter how much she wanted to drug them all just for the sake of having twelve hours undisturbed, unintruded-upon, blissfully alone, all to herself with no one in seeing, yelling, or smelling distance — no matter how seductive the temptation, she wouldn't do it. Not unless it came to a point where someone's life was in danger, or the *Jupiter Two* might be damaged.

Of course, an ounce of prevention always was worth a pound of cure. They told you that in med school, over and over and over until you thought you'd go mad. But it really was true, never so much so as in an emergency unit on a Saturday night in the middle of a big city, even one with domes like Houston's.

The thought of her time spent interning at the med center emergency room brought on a rush of homesickness as palpable as the effect of any drug. It caught her unprepared, and the tears spilled down her cheeks before she could will them not to. *God. Maybe the kindest thing would be giving everyone injections,* she thought. Put them to sleep and keep them asleep until finally, the respiratory reflex was suppressed enough to fade away. She could preside over each quiet passing before hooking herself up to an intravenous feed, which would do the same for her. An end to pain, both physical and psychological; no more waiting to see when the air could no longer be purified enough to be recycled, when the last of their nutrition could no longer be recovered, when the only water they could distill wouldn't fill a shot-glass for each of them. No, this would be much kinder, especially to Penny and Will.

And to herself. She could admit that. Why not? After all, what good was it to have been at the top of your profession when you ended up untold light-years away from anything that had to do with it, unable even to keep current, let alone improve? Who knew what they were doing back on Earth now in medicine, in biology, in the science of survival, regeneration, longevity? What year was it back there anyway? Was it possible to tell anymore, or were they lost in time as well as space, thanks to that godforsaken planet they'd crashed on? If you couldn't answer those questions, what difference did it make whether you lived or died?

When she found herself reaching toward the drawer where she kept the syringes and patches, she forced her hand to change direction, moving it to the cabinet over her desk where she kept the mood stabilizers. She hadn't told her parents that she had lately felt the need of chemical aids, and probably wouldn't. After all, she was an adult *and* a professional; whatever *professional* meant in this literal void, it still meant she was capable of making the right decisions for treatment, for herself as well as everyone else. She had studied this situation very carefully and she'd realized exactly when a course of stabilizers was called for. So far, she'd been doing pretty well. Not that her father would notice, of course.

Lately, though, it was getting harder. She'd have to up the dosage soon if things kept on the way they were — tension thick enough to make pea soup that would stand up to a spoon, or however the saying went.

As she was placing a stabilizer patch carefully on the back of her neck, under her hair, she heard her parents' voices become louder. They weren't fighting, she realized; they were excited. Almost *happy*.

Something someone had seen on the navigational unit, out in the interstellar wastes? Something detected on a sensor —

Judy found she was holding her breath. She didn't dare hope — didn't *dare*. Because if she did, and it turned out to be more nothing, she didn't think she could stand it; she might not be able to force her hand away from that drawer again.

Then they were calling her name and she was running through the *Jupiter Two* toward the bridge, to where Maureen and John were now laughing and crying and calling everyone to come quickly. Even that wretched Zachary Smith.

Chapter Two

John Robinson felt better. Maybe not better than he'd ever felt in his life, but pretty close, and worlds away (you should pardon the expression) from the caged and beaten cabin-fever malaise of what was nothing less than waiting to die.

When the sensors had first picked up the presence of the world-sized object, emitting unmistakable signs of life in this starless vacuum where no life should have been possible, he had felt something in his being *jump* with exhilaration. He knew the technical explanation by heart — adrenaline this, endorphins that. But actually experiencing the *rush* of it felt a lot bigger and more significant than mere brain chemicals reacting. He glanced at Don West, sitting to his left. *OK, hotshot, I think I've had a taste of what makes you go.* At this moment, he could almost wish the *Jupiter Two* was some kind of sleek fighter craft, something they could whip around the enormous *thing* hanging in the Big Black in front of them. Now he *wanted* to be alive — not just wanted, *insisted* on it. He would never again allow that malaise to settle over him; no more marking time, treading water. It was as if the enormous sphere had come out of nowhere to remind him, in the words of the old poem, that life was real, life was earnest —

And then again, he could be getting a little drunk with all the excitement, too, he thought, a bit wryly. "Readings, Maureen?" he asked.

"It's not alive but there are definitely life-forms in it," she said. "As well as energy levels that suggest lifeforms in residence there, on a long-term basis."

Don looked over at him. "Someone else lost in space? Only that group is bigger than our group."

"Not lost," Will said. "The rate of travel indicates there's a destination in mind."

"A destination would figure," Judy said, thoughtfully. She was bent over the same part of the console with Maureen, entering data on an electronic clipboard with one hand and tapping the library screen with the other. "I mean, there would have to be. Most of the life-forms inside this thing register as sentient. Conscious." She looked up at John. "Intelligent — which is to say, human, or human equivalent."

"Call it human," John said.

"Isn't that kind of chauvinistic?" Penny said. "I mean, maybe they have their own word for it and we're *that-word* equivalent. If you see what I mean."

"I do," John said, talking over the smart remark Will was about to make. "And I'm counting on you to learn their language well enough that we can use their word as a translation of *human* in the proper context. So we won't sound like chauvinists." He looked back at her and winked. “Capice?”

“ ’Peesh,” she said, smiling for the first time in who knew how long.

“Orbit calculated,” Don said. “Beginning the five-dollar tour.”

John leaned over the magnification screen and studied the close-up of the object’s surface. In general, it wasn’t as rough or pitted as he’d imagined it would be, though in spots it appeared to have been sandblasted with industrial diamonds. He couldn’t see anything like structural damage; either they hadn’t met a certain breed of metal-eating spider or they had a foolproof repellent.

“More people in the center, it would seem, than anywhere else,” Maureen said.

“More protection,” Don said reasonably and then frowned. Coming up along the planet’s curve was an enormous area of lines that seemed to have been etched into the surface — deliberately etched. The pattern reminded John of something he’d seen in South America, the giant lines and designs that certain squish-heads were sure marked out landing fields for the chariots of the god-aliens.

If this was one of those chariots, however, those landing fields were too small by far. This was perhaps three-quarters the size of the Earth’s moon, though its mass was a great deal less.

“What’s *that* supposed to be?” Don said. It was easy enough to see without magnification, a lopsided arrangement of overlapping rectangles, octagons, oblongs, and ellipses.

"What does it look like?" John asked him.

Don laughed a little. "Beats the hell out of me. I never could understand any of that modern art stuff on Earth, never mind stuff from another planet."

"Tribal?" guessed Maureen. "Or perhaps their version of an identifying number, a serial numbers?"

"A brand name," Will said. "Maybe *their* Coca-Cola sponsored *their* mission, too."

"A billboard," Judy said. "Eat at Joe's. Or, Eat at UFO's."

"A bumper sticker," said Don. "If you can read this, you're too damned close."

"A target."

They all turned to look at Penny, who was sketching briskly in her diary/archiver. She looked back at them evenly, her attention chiefly on John.

"Just look at it. A lot of the shapes overlap in the same spot, and even those that don't seem to be pointing at it."

"I don't see that," Judy said slowly, but not in an argumentative way.

"I do," Don said. "She's right."

"A *target?*" Will said, incredulously. "Like — for *what?*"

"Pin the Tail on the Alien." John turned to see Smith standing in the entryway with his arms folded, looking sleepily malevolent.

"We could pin a tail on you instead," said Don, his eyes on the console. "That would be a step *up* the evolutionary ladder for you."

"Don't confuse me with your relatives," Smith said disdainfully.

"At least mine are vertebrates."

"Do you two *ever* quit?" Judy's voice was exasperated, though John thought he detected a hint of a laugh.

"I've tried," Smith said. "I turned in my resignation long ago but I can't seem to catch a life *off* this safari."

"Well, who knows, Smitty," Don said, making some adjustments on the console. "This could be your chance."

"What do you mean?" John asked him.

"Penny's 'target.' " Don paused. "As in, 'This way in, folks. Enter here.' " He looked at John expectantly.

"Let's take one more spin around the joint," said John. "I want to see what the exit looks like."

"I think that's it. Entrance *and* exit together."

"Maybe. But if so, I don't like it."

"Why not?" Don asked him.

"Because I don't like places that have only one way in and out."

"Very wise, Dr. Robinson," Smith said. "If whatever is in there is alive, then it needs sustenance. Or, to put it in words short enough for the major to understand, *food.* Perhaps human flesh isn't their favorite dish, but out here it probably doesn't pay to be too choosy."

"Thank you for that thought," Maureen murmured.

Don suddenly got up and went over to him, before he could run back to his quarters. "OK, *Smitty,*" he said with exaggerated cheerfulness, "tell you what. We'll offer you to them as an hors d'oeuvre, and if they snap you up and ask for more, we'll know it's time to start worrying."

Smith's expression hardened. "Don't call me Smitty, *Donny.*"

Don started to make a move — either a gesture, or maybe getting ready to throw a punch. John raised his voice. "Major West, return to your post. You don't have permission to leave it."

The look on Don's face was unreadable, but he did as he was told. Smith sneered at his back. When he got to his chair, however, he stood looking down at the console screen in disbelief, and then up at the sphere, visible through the blast-shield.

"You and Penny were right," John told him.

"Yeah, I can see that," Don said. The area where so many of the shapes overlapped was slowly irising open in an unmistakable invitation. "You think that's for us?"

"You see any other spacecraft hanging around this part of the universe?" Judy asked.

"What makes you think we'd *see* anything like that?" said Smith. "We didn't *see* this till it was nearly on top of us."

"I didn't have the sensors set for that kind of distance," John said, "so don't go all spooky about it."

"I'm spooky enough for you, I'm sure," Smith said, sounding as nasty as ever. It figured that this new development would do nothing for his disposition. Not that John had really expected it to. He'd been tempted, now and again, to force Smith into hibernation, even though it probably would have been a death sentence. Somehow, he just hadn't been able to bring himself to do it. But if the wretch kept it up, he would probably find it in himself to march the miserable being into one of the capsules at gunpoint.

Or he might let Don do it. Don would enjoy it, mainly because Smith was so scared of him.

"Never mind," he said. "Once more around, Major."

There was a pause. "I'm afraid I won't be able to comply." Don's voice had an edge of anticipation.

"Evasive maneuvers?" John asked without much hope.

For answer, Don played his fingers over the console as if it were a musical keyboard. "Even manual override is gone."

"Well, I wish I could say it's been a pleasure," Smith said, and then gave a short, humorless laugh. "Actually, I don't. I'd tell you to give my regards to oblivion, but it seems I'll be able to do that myself."

Before anyone could answer, John heard the

elevator power up from the level below.

"Holy cow!" yelled Will.

"Robot is online," said the familiar mechanical voice. John realized it had actually been some time since he'd last heard it. Will had been tearing it down and rebuilding it over and over, trying to make some kind of breakthrough with parallel processing.

The elevator platform came to a stop and the robot rolled itself forward onto the bridge.

"It's so nice," Smith said acidly, "that we can *all* be together at the end."

"Dad," Will said shakily, "I took out the power source."

John looked at Don West and then at Maureen.

"Will Robinson is correct," said the robot. *"Robot is temporarily powered by remote source. Translation underway."*

"Explain," John said.

"Power source provider will provide translation and translating devices based on information gathered here."

"Indeed," John said; a light feeling of vertigo was sweeping over him, getting stronger.

"Indeed." Smith's echo was mocking. "And then what?"

The robot rotated in his direction. *"Then we eat."*

Chapter Three

Chin resting on her fists, Penny stared at the small screen in the arm of Don West's chair, dangling her legs eight feet above the bridge as she contemplated the object that the *Jupiter Two* was slowly approaching. She had been sitting up there for over an hour, ever since Judy had finally sedated Dr. Smith and locked him in his quarters. There wasn't a whole lot else to do except watch the opening in the big metal ball grow larger and larger, and, in between working on the file her mother had given her, finish her cycle of Dream Dancer poems. Perhaps she might have time to stick a chip from the archiver in a capsule and launch it into space, like a message in a bottle. Maybe someday someone would find it and be able to decode all the links and spots so they could get the full multimedia presentation of the last Star Songs of the Dream Dancer.

If Dr. Smith was right, of course, and this was the end for all of them. It was entirely possible, however, that it wasn't.

Why would anyone, even an alien, a really *alien* alien, more alien even than the Blawp, currently sleeping peacefully in hibernation, bother sending them messages through the robot if they were just going to be killed? A waste of time. And if they were going to be killed, they could just as easily have been killed immediately, she thought. Anything that could take control of the ship and the robot to such an extent was capable of shutting off the air and suffocating them, or even gassing them with any of the noxious things that combined to make fuel.

She leaned over the side of the chair and watched the rest of her family. Will was busy trying to run a diagnostic on the robot and getting contradictory readings almost every minute. Or was that a diagnostic? Maybe he was trying to trace the power, see how it was being transmitted, or projected.

He wasn't having much luck, but information was still flooding into the life sciences databanks. Her mother and Judy were poring over it, trying to organize it. Some of it, Judy said, seemed to be the same thing in a dozen different languages or codes. The file Penny herself was working on was something her mother had given her, a chunky mess of information that reminded her of what used to happen generations ago when people tried to download binary files from networks and got pages and pages and pages of garble because they opened it into a word processor or a drawing program.

Penny had fed the pile into the archiver, crossing her fingers that the quarantine mode would hold. Either it did, or there was nothing to quarantine in it, but the whole thing came out as music.

At least, she was pretty sure it was music. Judy

had been skeptical. Don West had said he thought it was a video track decoded improperly, but Penny stubbornly insisted that it was music. Why not? Maybe aliens didn't call it music exactly, or maybe music filled a different purpose for them. But anything involving sound and/or vibration she was going to call music until someone came up with something better.

Of course, that was the archiver's take on it, what the archiver thought it most closely resembled as input. The archiver could have been wrong — it was, after all, just a recording and decoding device. It didn't have even a rudimentary electronic mind, let alone something on the level of the robot's. Maybe she could try reformatting the data after she finished this section of what might or might not be the final Star Songs of the Dream Dancer.

The chair gave a small jerk and began to descend slowly.

"Twenty seconds to entry into spacecraft of unknown origin," Don said, standing at the console. He looked up at her apologetically. "Everyone assume their regular stations. And if there's a chance in hell I can seize control of the *Jupiter Two* at some point, I will."

"What for?" Penny said as she reached his eye level. "This might be the only source of breathable air, not to mention food and water, for a gazillion light-years."

"It depends on how important that is to you," Don said, lowering the chair completely. "I'd rather we kept breathing on our own terms, and not someone else's."

"What's the difference?" asked Penny. "Alive is alive, dead is dead."

"There's alive on a nice spring day out in the country, and there's alive in the bowels of a Turkish prison," Don said. "You tell me what the difference is."

"I can't," Penny said stubbornly. "Those both disappeared before I was born." She went to the Video Mechanics station and belted in.

Zachary Smith woke with a light flickering in his eyes. Blinking, he raised up on one elbow, trying to remember anything, anything at all, and couldn't. The only thing he knew for sure was that he must still be on the accursed *Jupiter Two*, and he was not waking from a sweet session of the Kiss, because his head hurt like hell — *two* hells.

He pushed himself slowly to a sitting position and winced as his feet touched the floor. The headache was actually all over his body. What in the name of God — ?

The source of the flickering light swam into overly sharp focus: the monitor screen above his desk. The Robinsons had very thoughtfully piped in the view from the bridge monitors so he could share the experience of being captured and eaten (or something) by aliens who would probably make metal-eating spiders look like puppies.

"Lovely," he said, watching the metal entry

hole swell until there was nothing else on the screen. He shuffled over to the desk and pressed the communications panel. "Thanks awfully for the show, but I'd rather not watch this movie, if it's all the same to you. Turn off my monitor."

"It *is* all the same to me," came John Robinson's voice in response, "but we didn't turn your monitor on."

"Apparently our hosts don't want you to miss one thrilling moment, *Smitty*," added Don West. "So why don't you just sit back, put your feet up, and shut your mouth?" The speaker went dead. Smith pushed on the panel a couple of times but nothing happened. On the monitor screen, the darkness suddenly resolved itself into a fairly well lit cavern, or tunnel, with lights stretching far into the distance in dotted parallel lines.

He moved closer to the screen and something very much like a bolt of lightning with sharp spikes all over it went through the top of his head into his eye sockets. Oh God, *now* he knew what the trouble was.

Moving carefully but not too quickly, for fear that his head might explode, Smith found his made-up supply of Kiss on the nightstand and sucked a dose out of the eyedropper. The thirty seconds before it began to take effect were the longest Smith had ever spent. But after that, of course, it didn't matter. Nothing did, except making sure he would have his entire made-up supply on him at all times.

Said supply came to all of three bottles, which he reckoned was about three weeks' worth. Raw materials, the ingredients, where were they? He scrabbled the packages of antihistamines and amino acids out of the lower drawer, hesitated, and then stuck them down the back of his pants. Okay, now he was ready for just about anything.

He went back to look at the monitor. The light level had shifted again and it was hard to see exactly what their surroundings looked like, other than those long trails of lights, but they appeared to have arrived at some sort of landing pad. Was it lifting up to meet the *Jupiter Two*, or was the ship descending to it?

A little of both, he decided, sitting down carefully. Might as well watch the rest of the show, he thought. He was prepared. And who knew — alien was alien, but he was willing to bet that even aliens embraced the concept of gratification. Or, putting it a bit more accurately, getting stoned. Was there ever a culture that didn't have a niche for a drug dealer?

Hell, no.

The bump of contact was almost too soft to be perceptible, but Judy felt it in every part of her body, and she could tell just by looking around that the rest of them had felt it the same way. The silence among them was suddenly so enormously and powerfully loud that she wasn't sure if she would ever hear anything again.

Then Penny's voice cut through the roaring silence, as clear and bright as an icicle. "Are we there yet?"

Chapter Four

An hour later, they were all still sitting at their stations on the bridge, while the robot stood near the navigation unit, clicking and whirring to itself. Will had persuaded his father to allow him to examine the robot, but as soon as he had approached it, it had extended its arm to ward him off, intoning, *"Danger, Will Robinson, danger!"* He couldn't see any danger, and he knew the robot could not have been either magnetized or charged because it was still functioning, but he backed off anyway and tried to keep track of the various states it seemed to be fluctuating through.

He knew that at times it was receiving information from some source outside the *Jupiter Two*, though at other times it seemed as if the ship's own databanks were feeding it information it had not had access to before.

It would also go through strange periods of very high speed transmission in some completely unfamiliar machine language. He assumed it was machine language, anyway, even if it did sound an awful lot like birds on amphetamines.

Then there was a state where the robot seemed to be talking to itself, and listening intently to what it was saying. Will couldn't decide what that might indicate, whether the robot was trying to memorize something or perhaps was echoing aloud both halves of a dialogue it was having with some other intelligence, machine or otherwise.

Whatever was happening to the robot, the new arrangement of processors Will had designed seemed to be up to the job. The robot was handling more complex transactions in greater numbers. If only he could have had access to more resources than the dwindling supply on the *Jupiter Two* — he might have been able to shield it from whatever was interfering with it right now.

Abruptly, as if he'd said something, the robot swiveled around to face him. After a pause, it turned toward Penny, and then his mother, and then to each of the others. As if it were imprinting their faces in its memory — or transmitting their images?

"Translation complete," the robot said, and there was something new in its mechanical voice, something that made Will think of a person talking through a machine rather than a machine talking. He wasn't just imagining it, either — he could see that Penny and his mother had heard it as well. Goose bumps swam up the back of his neck and tingled briefly in his hair. Was the robot still a robot — still *his* robot?

Then he heard the outer door open and his stomach dropped just the way it used to when he would go up one of the Houston skystalks in the express elevator — two hundred stories in two hundred seconds, or whatever it was. He turned and met Penny's gaze. She was almost smiling and he realized that his expression was identical. Whatever happened next would be nothing compared to the relief it would bring.

At first Will thought he was hallucinating the thing that rolled onto the *Jupiter Two* bridge. Then he saw the strange half-circles of metal wagging from side to side on that very familiar limb as the machine moved toward his father, and he knew that it wasn't an illusion. Whoever or whatever was meeting them had deliberately built this thing to look exactly like their own robot. Whoever, he decided; whoever, not whatever. It took a human type of intelligence to come up with an idea like that. Copying something visitors were already familiar with to show them you understood, were on roughly the same level, and meant no harm, was most definitely the province of human beings. His gaze slid to Penny as she accepted one of the half-circles from the machine and put it on her head. Like a headband?

No, stupid, he chided himself. *Like* earphones. *Earphones to hear in translation.*

He took the next-to-last pair of earphones and the robot trundled away from him, heading toward Smith's quarters. But Smith was already in the entryway, looking bleary, like a guy with a hangover on a morning after that wasn't quite finished being the night before.

"I thought the entertainment portion of our journey had concluded," Smith said thickly.

The new robot pushed the earphones at him

and he jumped back, noticing that there were two robots for the first time. "Where'd you get the other one?" he demanded.

"It's either an incredible coincidence or a peace offering," Will said, fitting the earphones to his head and looking at his father.

His father, already wearing his earphones, nodded at him, his expression apprehensive. "Either way, I hope you're right, Will."

"In one way, he is right," said a new voice, coming through the duplicate robot's speaker. The speaker was the sort that Penny had had on her entertainment system back on Earth, except the sound quality seemed to be even better. The voice was deep in tone and musical, and could have been either male or female. *"And may I say that a synonym for 'determination' is quite a fine name for someone? Yet to call another in the same clan by the title of the lowest coin for transaction seems somehow counterproductive?"*

Will looked at Penny and couldn't help smirking. "*Obviously* a very highly developed civilization. I think you're in for a rough ride here, Sis."

His father made shushing gestures at him. "This is an oddity of our language we can explain," he said, speaking slowly and carefully. "So to whom shall we explain it?"

"Who are you *talking* to?" Smith demanded angrily. He was still holding the earphones in one hand, looking bewildered and a bit nauseated.

"Put the earphones on," Judy told him.

Smith obeyed. Then he looked around. "So? Well? What am I supposed to hear?"

"The ocean, Smith," Don said. "Oh no, wait, I forgot, it's the other way round — if I held your head up to my ear, *I'd* hear the ocean."

Will smothered a laugh. Smith glared at the pilot. "*You'd* hear the ocean no matter *what* you held up to your ear, you nattering Neanderthal."

"And why," said the voice from the robot's speaker, *"does this one not know the full nature of the challenge?"*

Smith actually jumped. Will saw his father look at him, and then at Don and Judy with something like amusement. "Maybe because none of us realized it, either."

"Now we should eat," said the voice. *"Do your customs permit you to leave this enclosure?"*

Will couldn't help it. Suddenly the prospect of being anywhere but inside the *Jupiter Two* was too much to resist. He raced for the exit even as his parents were calling for him to wait.

Chapter Five

The first thing Maureen noticed about the alien standing over her son sprawled on the floor was that paintbox sky-blue skin. The dull, off-white pajama-style garment it wore made its skin seem even more luminous in comparison.

Then her protective instincts kicked in and she wanted to rush forward and push the alien away from Will, throw herself between it and him, draw her weapon and blow it to hell. She took a step forward just as the creature bent down and wrapped its long, graceful fingers around Will's upper arms.

"Hands," Judy breathed, in wonder or in relief, Maureen couldn't tell which. Possibly both. "Hands, with five fingers and opposable thumbs. We're definitely relatives, or as good as."

"Not so fast," Smith said, standing on Judy's other side. "You can say the same for chimpanzees, and they've got twice as many opposable thumbs as we do." He paused for a moment. "Them, and Major West."

Maureen looked back to Will, who was on his feet now. The alien still had its — his? her? — graceful hands on his shoulders, as if to feel his texture, or his temperature. It — he? she? — could have passed for human, except for that blue skin. The long hair had been twisted into a mass of coils, which were held back, for the moment, by earphones identical to the ones she and the others were wearing.

She looked past the creature, down the tunnel, or whatever it was, where the lines of light eventually curved down and out of sight, and saw no one else, no squad of soldiers or police or the equivalent. Had this creature really come alone to meet them?

The alien turned from Will to face her. Oriental features? More like Polynesian? Maori? She thought she could see a hint of each there and suspected that the resemblances might well shift with her perspective until she got used to the sight. Assuming all the inhabitants were blue and of the same origin. They might not be. Certainly, they didn't have to be —

The alien moved toward her, raising both hands as if to surrender. "Your proximity is not only tolerated but welcomed. Hello."

The words she heard in her earphones didn't match the movements of the alien's thin-lipped mouth. She hoped the voice was authentic, though. It was the same musical bass contralto that had come from the duplicate robot's speaker.

"This," Maureen said, tapping her earphones, "is quite a gadget."

The alien's eyes were a uniform black with no whites and no irises that Maureen could see. They also seemed to be dry rather than moist.

The eyelids never blinked. "A legacy from the first visitors anyone remembers. The accounts say that the visitors' world was as large as ours, but failing. They wanted to speak and listen, and taught these machines to help them do so. Those machines taught us how to make more." The alien's shiny black gaze went to the two robots.

"Your machine has taught us about you-the-people, and shown us much more that we don't understand." Now the alien was looking at the *Jupiter Two.* "We had no idea that any intelligent creatures could exist in such an extremely small world. Is there something in your scents that prevents proximity madness?"

Maureen hesitated. "My, but we have a great deal to talk about," she said finally. Only later would she remember how she had thought, for some reason, that the alien had said *sense* rather than *scents.*

Don walked a few paces behind the group as they followed the alien into the tunnel, just behind the twin robots. He kept far enough back that he had elbow room to deal with anything that might suddenly come at them from the rear, but not so far that he could be easily cut off from the rest of them — say, by a couple of robots with unsuspected programming. So far, the two machines showed no sign of doing anything other than rolling along behind the humans. If they were aware of each other, it didn't show. But they wouldn't be unless they were ordered to; it was like expecting two cans of soup to be aware of each other.

It was all peaceful enough — nothing like the last time they'd boarded another spacecraft — but it sure was *weird.* Watching those alien lips move out of synch with the words he heard through the earphones was like watching one of those old nondigital movies. He'd gone to a festival for antique entertainment buffs with a girl he'd been chasing, on the promise of a promise that she would warm up to him more if he showed an interest. He'd ended up sitting in a dark room with five hundred other people, all of them compulsively crunching popcorn and candy bars, staring at front projections of old dramas. Some of the dramas — movies, to use the old term — had been originally made in a foreign language and the voices had been *dubbed* in English. It had been so weird to watch the mouths go one way while the words went another. The whole time, he hadn't been able to shake the feeling that what he was hearing didn't always have a lot to do with what the people on the screen were actually saying — not then, and not now.

How could any culture, no matter how advanced, build working translators for a language they'd never encountered before? It should have been impossible. He didn't have to be the smartest guy in the group to know that. Not that he was as stupid as that ratbag Sleazel Smith made him out to be. As Jeb always used to say, knowing that you weren't the smartest guy in the place was a sure sign that you weren't the dumbest, either.

So how *did* those translators work? Did Big Blue, up there in the lead, have any idea, or was the alien only a pawn?

Under his feet, he could feel the tunnel sloping downward, the curve becoming gradually steeper until it leveled off and the alien brought them to a stop. Now they were standing on a wide ledge — no, a platform, like a subway platform. They huddled together, Don moving casually back and forth so it wouldn't look as if he were making sure no one strayed or was pulled out of the group suddenly.

This was apparently a nexus of tunnels; the lines of light diverged in all directions, making bizarre interior constellations all identical to one another. Don tried to estimate how deep inside the sphere they might be. Not very deep, he thought, not close to the inner axis. Perhaps the transport and communication lines ran near the surface, enveloping the living area. You'd get better coverage that way, he supposed, although you'd have a hell of a lot more distance to work on. He wondered how they'd managed to get all that work done, or even if they had. The memory of an old history lesson about how the Chinese had worked on the railroads in the U.S. during the nineteenth century flitted through his mind, making him even more uneasy.

He sensed movement before he saw the dark

shape blocking out some of the lights; the air pressing against his eardrums. Then there was a whiff of something oily, and an object similar in shape to a boxcar, only quite a bit smaller, slid into place next to the platform with a pneumatic sigh.

A boxcar? Try a subway car, old-timer. Don allowed himself a moment of amusement at his unexpectedly quaint turn of thought, then remembered the Chinese in nineteenth-century America again. Feeling even more uneasy, he stepped into the transport with everyone else and took a seat facing the entrance, one hand on his weapon. As if he knew anything about that old American custom of riding the rails. Or subways, come to think of it.

Maybe, he thought grimly, he should have studied up on both.

The trip was smooth, with only a few minor and very gentle bumps — how Judy imagined it must have been to travel in a zeppelin on a very calm day, even if this was underground. The light inside the car reminded her of the antique lamp she'd had in her bedroom back on Earth. It was a genuine art-deco era brass floor lamp and she had left it in the care of her old med school roommate, telling her not to lose it or sell it, because she would be back for it someday.

She suppressed the mournful nostalgia threatening to well up inside of her and concentrated on her surroundings. The seats were built in all around the inside perimeter, unpadded and made for a form a bit more tubelike than a standard human, if the molded back was anything to judge by, not to mention that alien. The soft light came from small sconces set into the walls at her standing eye level.

Her gaze came to rest on the blue creature again. It hadn't given a name yet, or asked theirs, though names were a sure thing in any culture that recognized individuals. Maybe a name was extremely private, even intimate, something that was bound up with the idea of proximity. Maybe names here weren't even verbal. Maybe a name could only be expressed in body language?

Were these translator earphones all they appeared to be, or was there less here than met the ear, so to speak?

She hadn't seen the alien's ears yet; they were completely covered by the headphones, so she had no idea if they bore any resemblance to human ears, even just on the outside. And as for the alien's eyes — just how and what did the creature see with those dark, dry organs?

She wondered what the local customs were regarding medical examinations and scientific curiosity. They spoke of their learning process as being taught, so they couldn't be too opposed to those ideas. Could they?

The worst part, Smith thought, was the eyes. Like two pieces of coal jammed into that flat, blue face. He was willing to bet that the skin color was artificially produced, no more natural than silver dreadlocks on a media celeb. But *those eyes* — God, what *were* they? Two pieces of black quartz chipped off some boulder — a comet or a meteorite, maybe? He hadn't thought those eyes were real organs of sight, but then he had actually seen them *move.* Sickening. And he'd never been all that squeamish, certainly — you couldn't be squeamish and maintain a practice as a doctor, after all. But having actually watched those . . . *organs* . . . moving up and down, from one side to another, and never ever blinking — it turned his stomach. Though for the life of him, he could not have said why.

Perhaps he should pretend to be tired or ill, or both. You never knew but that giving offense could be fatal here. It could be fatal in plenty of places on Earth, where eyes were eyes and blue was for skies, not skin, so who knew about here? All told, it would probably be better not even to talk if he could possibly help it.

He started to cross his legs and then winced. He'd forgotten about the impromptu hiding place for the Kiss ingredients. Maureen Robinson had noticed; she raised her eyebrows at him questioningly. He did what he could to look as if he were pretending he didn't feel ill.

"Something wrong, Smith?"

John Robinson was staring at him, one eyebrow raised in his characteristic expression of suspicion.

"Slight cramp," Smith said and sat back in the

just-slightly-too-narrow seat. "I'm sure I'll be fine."

"I'm sure, too," Don West said, sitting forward to look at him. "And you'll be good, too. Won't you, Smitty?"

"Don't call me Smitty."

Judy put a hand in the middle of Don West's chest and gently pushed so that he sat back. She shook her head, glancing significantly at the alien and then turning to him, her face tense with apprehension.

For a moment, he actually wanted to comfort her in some way, reassure her, say something encouraging. Instead he deliberately bit his tongue and looked away. Dr. Judith Robinson was hardly the sort of person who needed her hand patted, metaphorically or otherwise — even if he could have thought of something to say.

And now that blue *thing* was watching him with those revolting coal-lump eyes. At least, he thought it was watching him. Its face was turned toward him and those disgusting protuberances were moving up and down, up and down, as if taking his measurement continuously. Forcing himself not to squirm, he pretended great interest in the rather unimaginative interior and found that now everyone was staring at him, except for Penny, who was pouting at the floor, or the toes of her ridiculous velvet shoes.

"Is there something you people want from me?" he said at last.

"You won't be *happy* in the same place," the

alien said, except the word *happy* came out sort of fuzzy and slurred.

"I won't be *what?*" Smith said, astounded in spite of himself.

"That happens when the translator is using a meaning that is not as close as it should be. The word sounds odd."

"I'm sure I don't know what you mean," Smith said firmly. He leaned his head back and closed his eyes. With any luck, he might actually fall asleep and possibly miss the next several hours until it was time for his next Kiss.

The transport slid to a halt; a moment later, there was the sound of a lock disengaging. Will couldn't help shuddering. The door was going to open and they were going to see . . . *something.* Terror rushed through him like a cold, swiftly flowing river, making perfect sense to him in a way he couldn't explain without sounding classically stupid. It was like the time he'd taken his first look through a microscope. The fear had come from out of nowhere, conjured out of nothing by nothing. He'd had no idea what had brought it on, except that he was suddenly terrified at the idea of looking through the microscope. Not even an electron microscope, or a feed from MicroNet, but a plain, old-fashioned, manual desktop triple-lensed, one-eyed microscope that had been in use forever. Will could not have explained it to anyone — especially not his mother or Judy, the organic scientists in the family. He thought it was loony himself.

Now the fear was back, and it had less to do with the possible danger of cooperating with this being, and allowing it to lead them into something that might turn out to be fatal. That certainly was a part, but it wasn't all, or even most, of why he was afraid.

It's just scary. *Seeing. Sometimes seeing is too scary* —

Then the door opened, and he *was* looking at it, straight at it, unable to look away.

At least, he thought dazedly, it wasn't a great big group of vicious, fanged, metal-eating spiders or mutated bacteria billions of fumes larger than the usual variety.

In fact, he thought with a sigh, it was almost disappointing.

An indoor city.

Penny's eyes widened and she wished she'd brought her archiver. She would have to commit her observations strictly to memory and hope she could remember the ones she had worded particularly well so she could record the whole experience later. Only, when *would* they get back to the *Jupiter Two*? In an hour, a day? A month?

No, she wouldn't be able to stand that, she thought, stepping out of the transport thing onto another platform. A month was too soon to go back to the *Jupiter Two. Six* months was too soon. There was no way — *no way* — anyone was going to force her back into that tin can now that she was here — wherever here was. Didn't matter. It was an indoor city, probably a million times the size of Houston, somewhere in space, and God, was it *beautiful.*

She was drinking in the sight from a tower deck surrounded by what she would have called a bazaar if she'd been back in a comfort dome on Earth. But then, she actually *was* in a comfort dome, the biggest comfort dome anyone had ever heard of. Anyone from Earth, she corrected herself, and turned to the alien.

The alien was watching the rest of her family react to the sight of the multicolored, glowing tents, some of them actually nothing more than diaphanous veils of material hung over brightly shining poles. She could see movement. People? More aliens? Robots? They moved along the paths between and around the tented areas, though from two hundred feet up, she couldn't tell what they were doing.

Oh, for crying out loud — what does anybody *do in a city? They're* shopping. *All intelligent life* shops. *The need to shop is what distinguishes us from animals.* She covered a smile with one hand. Will would have a positive conniption if she repeated that blasphemy to him. But it had to be true. Otherwise, this place wouldn't look so much like a *mall.*

John Robinson stepped back from the glass wall (maybe glass, maybe not, but he didn't have a better word yet) and observed Maureen, and then his younger daughter. *Please,* he implored Penny silently, *please pay attention, please see more than pretty lights and colors.*

In one way, he knew he was being unfair to his daughter. In another, he knew it was asking too much of an adolescent who had been locked up in too small a space with an unchanging roster for too long. The sight of something other than black, empty space and the *Jupiter Two* even had him feeling somewhat lightheaded. Without the iron self-control he'd been practicing for the last eight or nine months so that he wouldn't lose it and do something bizarre and awful, he might be hysterical by now.

At last, being repressed, uptight, and middle class finally turn out to be optimal survival traits. What would Penny say if he pulled her aside and told her that?

Maureen was looking at him, her face flushed with emotion — mixed emotions, if he knew his wife. "Remind you of anything?" he asked her.

"A comfort dome," she said. "It's like — no, it *is* a giant comfort dome."

"That's what *I* was thinking," Penny said, sounding

"Oh wow, *really?*" said Will. "What an incredibly radical kind of idea. *I* never would have thought of that. How'd you *ever* hit on *that* one?"

"I'm ignoring you." Penny put her back to him. "That's what it is, Mom. It's a comfort dome in space."

"You understand what that means," Maureen

said, her gaze moving from Penny back to John.

He nodded. "This was built for living."

"Uh, Dad," said Will, "no offense, but is whatever Penny's got *catching?* I mean, it's not like that isn't obvious."

John smiled at his son. Maureen had often remarked that Will's gigantic intellect could be like an overly large pair of shoes he still had to grow into, and there would be times when it wouldn't help him understand the why behind the what.

"What we're saying, Will, is that this is a place made for living *but not traveling.* In other words, it *isn't* meant to be a spacecraft."

"And if it ever was," Maureen added, looking out over the indoor cityscape, "it isn't anymore. And hasn't been for quite a long time."

"Excuse me," said the alien, and John jumped. He'd actually forgotten the creature was still there. "What is a 'spacecraft'?"

For a long moment, they were all silent. Then Judy cleared her throat.

"Why don't we eat first?"

Chapter Six

"We have several volumes of legends in our library," said the glowing woman. "Many tell of a past universe where tribes existed on the convex side of a sphere, in enchanted bubbles."

Don stared, the bland mixture that translated as *food* forgotten on the plate in front of him. He wasn't sure what he was most amazed at: that this alien was absolutely identifiable as a woman, that she really was glowing, or that John Robinson was sitting next to her listening and nodding as if there was nothing out of the ordinary.

Well, John Robinson was just one of those guys with that kind of cool, Don decided. Your basic poker-faced, world-saving, quick-thinking Boy Scout usually found in the diplomacy biz. *Us grunts who gotta go from zero to sixty with no warning, we don't get to relax that way.*

It had actually been quite a long time since he'd been even close to being a grunt. If any real grunts had heard his thoughts, they'd have arranged a Special Delivery, a gag where someone phoned in some luckless, usually unpopular person as a raw recruit gone AWOL from some boot camp. After luring the victim to some public area, they'd watch from hiding as the MPs descended, wrapped the accused in a sticky jacket and carted him or her off to a stockade.

The worst part of the gag was not really that it could take as long as a week to get yourself extricated, but that the record of the arrest was a hell of a lot harder to get rid of than the sticky jacket.

So what kind of mean humor did they have in this oversized ball bearing, he wondered. And how would they all end up learning about it?

Judy poked his ribs with a hard finger. *"Eat,"* she whispered.

He nodded absently and stirred his mush with the spoon. Perfectly recognizable as a spoon — he wasn't sure whether to be surprised or not. Was there any reason that sitting at a table, eating food off plates with eating utensils shouldn't be a logical development among humanoid species? Even if good cuisine wasn't.

He thought that the most significant feature might be the fact that the table was round. Maybe it came out of the same sort of thinking that King Arthur of legend had been partial to, or it might be only the decor in this room in this woman's home. If it *was* her home — or was it some neutral place where they took strangers who came to town, or whatever this was?

Which brought him to his next question — if that weird-looking alien really didn't know what a spacecraft was, had there ever been any other visitors from the outside?

And just where did this inverted planet come from in the first place?

An intense wave of fatigue swept over him, leaving him beached with exhaustion. He wanted to shove his plate aside and put his head down on the table like a sleepy child. The only thing that really kept him from doing so was knowing that neither John Robinson nor that ratbag Smith would ever let him live it down.

He had another spoonful of whatever-it-was and forced himself to swallow instead of yawn.

"In these enchanted bubbles, the air held together by itself as long as the people were virtuous," the woman went on, "and not profligate or wasteful. But if they did not obey the rules set down for them by their ancestors to maintain the balance of their ecology, they would suffer. The air would poison them and their bodies would become foul and diseased. If they persisted in their evil ways, the air would dissipate altogether and they would die."

Maureen nodded, readjusting the headphone over her left ear. She had a sore spot just back of the lobe that she suspected was being irritated further by the pressure.

Sitting on the other side of the shining woman, she caught John's eye, wondering if he knew what she was thinking. He probably did, John would know more so than anyone else. This legend could have been the Earth's own story, or at least part of it. Inside enchanted domes of air, people who hadn't learned their lesson carelessly producing waste upon waste with no thought to how it could be disposed of in any useful way, behaving as if the necessities of life were magicked into being just because people wanted them and every resource was eternally self-renewing — where had she heard that story before? It seemed as if certain weaknesses were inherent to intelligent life, human or equivalent.

They had left the transport arrival platform in a classic elevator. The blue alien had listened attentively while Will gave it a short course on space travel, sublight, hyperspatial, and hyperspatial without gates. That bizarre face was impossible to read with certainty, but she couldn't get over the feeling that the alien simply didn't believe what Will was saying. That was hard for *her* to believe, but the more she watched the alien, the stronger the feeling became.

Still, it hardly made sense. How could a sentient lifeform that lived inside an environment drifting in space *not* know what a spacecraft was?

Their dinner hostess, however, didn't seem to suffer from the same sort of skepticism. Or did she? Maureen realized she actually didn't know. The subject had not yet been addressed directly. Then she couldn't help smiling at the turn her thoughts were taking. As if the Robinsons sat down at the dinner table to discuss cultural differences with aliens on a regular basis.

The woman had been waiting for them right outside the door of the elevator, which had taken them not to the level they had seen from the arrival platform but to some place below that, directly to this — well, apartment, for lack of a better word. Come to that, the whole world was an apartment building, though. Space condo, she thought, and pressed the earphone against the sore spot to keep from laughing.

The woman had greeted them with a sort of curtsy, and only after she had led them into this dining room did they realize that the blue-skinned alien was no longer with them. The robots had remained near the elevator, suddenly deactivated by no means any of the humans had been aware of.

"Now we eat," the woman had told them, and they had gathered around the table, already set and laid with this rather mediocre stuff, and spent more than a few minutes looking at each other, for reassurance, or clues, or for no real reason other to see how everyone else was taking this. She had to smile at that, as well. Twenty-four hours earlier, none of them had been able to bear the sight of anyone else; now they were all looking to each other for the comfort of familiarity.

John's gaze was on her as if he had been reading her thoughts, but the shining woman was speaking again.

"Eventually, there were so many evil people under the stars that all the air became poisonous, and the bubbles began to evaporate. One tribe understood what was going to happen because they had remained very virtuous. They did not want to die and begged the gods to rescue them."

"The gods?" Maureen asked.

"According to the legend," the woman said. "Which is from a more naive time, when people imagined scientific principles to be a sort of superrace of disembodied beings who took a personal interest in the welfare of the ordinary mortal. The gods, they say, had mercy on the virtuous and sent a message to the head of the tribe in a dream. The messenger told her about a gateway at the bottom of the world that would allow them entry to the inside. There they would find good air, lots of water, and plenty of resources to start over, so they would not have to die with the rest. But because of the offenses the evil ones had committed, the gods ruled that no one from that race would ever be allowed to live directly in sight of the stars again."

Maureen's gaze found John's again, but it was Penny who spoke up.

"One of our myths has to do with a flood that destroyed the world, except for a man named Noah and his family. He was told to build an ark big enough to carry his family and two animals of every species. It rained for forty days and forty nights so that water covered the entire world."

The glowing womans' expression was fascinated. "A whole world of *water.*"

"After the water went down — according to the story," Maureen said, "a rainbow appeared in the sky as a promise that the world would never again be destroyed by a flood. But that's only one flood story. There were several other great flood myths from various other cultures on

Earth, and many more worldwide disasters other than floods."

"A *flood* of water." The woman was obviously having a hard time getting her mind around the concept. Apparently nothing had ever sprung a leak inside this odd little shell. "It's quite an image. Whole cities submerged in water?"

"They wouldn't have been cities like yours," John said. "They'd have been much more primitive. No tall buildings, no power."

"It's just a myth," Penny said. "Some people believe it really happened, but most people think it's either an old story, or something that did happen on a much smaller scale and got blown up and exaggerated."

Now the glowing woman smiled. "We have a lot of conflicting beliefs here, too. Something else our worlds have in common."

"You acknowledge other worlds," John said. "And yet the . . . person . . . who met us claimed not to know what a spacecraft was."

"Those are mystics," the woman said dismissively. "They live in the skin and contemplate the nothing. They have for . . . well, since the First Mother found the gateway in and brought her tribe to the Promised Land."

"I *really* wish I'd brought my archiver," Penny said.

The woman smiled at her. "You're a scholar, of course. There's a repository, you can look up all the old stories."

"Charming," Smith said. Maureen all but

jumped; somehow, she had completely forgotten about him. But there he was, sitting on Judy's left (she was bracketed on the right by Don, and it was beginning to look to Maureen like the start of a rivalry which, under the circumstances, couldn't have been more absurd). "All this has been terribly interesting, but I need to use the facility."

The woman's face was blank. "We have many facilities. You can use any that don't endanger you, or us."

"The toilet," Smith said impatiently.

Her expression went from blank to disgusted. *"Oh.* You're one of *those."*

Maureen looked to John, caught between fear and the desire to laugh. Her mind was racing. They should have realized that in this type of closed-system society, there would be issues around waste and waste disposal, especially in light of the myth they had just heard. If those issues extended to some kind of serious body modification, things might be about to get very, very difficult for all of them.

If they agreed to undergo this modification, whatever it was, they might end up unable to survive anywhere else. If they refused, they might be ejected immediately — and possibly without the formality of being inside the *Jupiter Two.*

The woman turned suddenly to Maureen, the disgust in her face deepening. "Or is he one of those *animals* you spoke of, evolved, or surgically enhanced? Talks and walks upright, wears clothes, domesticated but not civilized?"

Maureen opened her mouth, desperately trying to think of something to say.

"*I'd* say she's just described you to a T." Don West said, leaning forward to look around Judy.

"On the contrary, Major, I believe she's got the two of us mixed up." Smith's tone was not as acid as it would have been; he was too nervous.

"Forgive me," John said quickly, reaching out to touch the woman's arm and then changing his mind. "I think we're all at a loss here."

Maureen shot him a warning look and mouthed *Be careful,* as the woman turned to him.

"How is *that?*" the woman asked him, bewilderment mixing with disgust.

"Perhaps our respective customs are . . . well, not different, just . . . well . . ." John hesitated. "Exactly what did this man do wrong?"

The silence that fell was intense, icy, and seemed to last an eternity.

"Now *I* am at a loss," the woman said finally. "Am I to believe that there are civilized people who speak of . . . of *that* . . . in the presence of *food?*"

Maureen felt her tension ease back a notch. "Apologize at once," she said to Smith. "You've made a mistake."

"I hardly think that one can apologize for being — ," the woman told her, still hostile. The final word had come out as hopeless garble. The woman watched all of them puzzling over it.

"You really have no word for that?"

"I guess not," said John. "We certainly don't mean to give offense."

"*Give* offense?" The woman's voice was incredulous. "You *are* offense." She pushed back from the table and stood up. "Someone else will see to your proper . . . disposition. As soon as possible, you are to leave this residence so that I can have it cleared, disinfected, and resanctified." She turned her hostile gaze to Maureen who was still staring at her open-mouthed. "And I had hoped that you and I . . ." She shuddered and stalked out.

"Nice going, Smitty," Don West said. "Anyone have any ideas on what we do now?"

"Just sit here and wait for the Potty Police, I guess," Will said, giving his father a worried look.

"Great," Penny said. "We make contact with another world and they think it's a crime to mention needing to go to the bathroom. I can tell this place is going to be a real party."

"Relax, relax," John said, holding his hand up for quiet. "Everybody calm down. You think we're the only people on Earth — from Earth — who ever had this problem?"

Maureen blinked at him. "I don't —"

"Everyone thought the Hopi Indians were degenerates of some kind because they kept tearing the toilets out of their government-supplied reservation homes, and putting them outside," he said. "No one asked the Hopis how they felt about indoor plumbing. If they had, the Hopis would have told them that they think having the toilet inside the house is a filthy thing." He paused for a moment, letting them think about it. "She also said, if you remember, that they have lots of conflicting beliefs here."

"You'd better hope some of those have to do with what's considered proper table talk," Don said gravely.

"So had you," said Judy. "And all the rest of us, too."

"But we're back to my original question," Don said, "which is, what now?"

"We wait," John said. "We wait, and for God's sake, try not to do anything rude while we're waiting."

Smith shifted uncomfortably in his chair. "Easy for you to say."

The robot appeared in the doorway; it was their own robot, Maureen saw, and not the copy. *"We are to leave. At once."*

"What, no 'Danger, danger!'?" Smith asked sourly.

John got up. "All right, all right. She said she wanted us out of here as soon as possible." He turned to the robot. "Where are we supposed to go?"

"The airlock," the robot told him.

Don West materialized next to John with his weapon drawn and ready. "Well, they're just going to have to come and get us."

The robot's dome lights flashed rapidly in a complicated sequence. *"They are."*

Chapter Seven

Eventually, Don's arm tired and he lowered his weapon to his side. "I thought you said they were coming," he said to the robot.

"They are," the robot told him.

"So where are they?"

"Still ten levels away."

"Which way — up or down?"

The robot didn't answer. Don turned to John and Maureen. "You think they're taking their time because they know we can't get out of here?"

John looked around the room. No doors, no windows, not even pictures. Just those strangely blank walls. Maybe the idea of an emergency exit was too absurd for an indoor society. Smith, still at the far side of the table, finally got up. "If I'm not mistaken," he said wearily, "I think there's a trapdoor over here."

Don ran around the table to have a look. "He might be right," he told the Robinsons. "There's something set into the floor here, looks like it opens." They all crowded around to see, except for Smith, who stood back behind Judy. If that ratbag didn't stop harassing her, Don thought, he was going to have to do something to him. He moved both hands quickly over the square panel on the floor, feeling for a latch or a button or anything that might be a release. Will scrambled forward to help, his smaller fingers prying at the outline of the square.

"No good," Don said. "It might not even be a trapdoor anyway." He stood up. "Okay, who's armed?"

John and Maureen had weapons, he saw, but not Judy. Another disadvantage: Aside from the fact that they could have used another weapon, Judy was actually a better shot than either of her parents. Don made a quick decision.

"Maureen, give your weapon to Judy and take charge of Penny, Will, and Smith."

Both John and Maureen started to protest.

"Don't argue!" he barked at them. "We're not on the *Jupiter Two* any more and this time it's *my* ass, it's *your* ass, it's *all* our asses!"

Before Maureen could move, he snatched the weapon away from her and thrust it at Judy.

"Now, get on the right side of the doorway and be ready to shoot whatever comes through it. No matter what else happens." Don stepped forward to give her a push but she was already in motion. Some instinct — strong drive to survive, Don thought — made her flatten herself against the wall and hold the weapon up and ready. Good girl. He turned to John Robinson.

"You get down on the far side of the table opposite the door and aim at the doorway, both arms on the table. Maureen, you and the kids get down out of sight under the table but near John. If he falls, you be ready to pick up where he left off. And you two" — he pointed at Will and Penny with his free hand — "you keep your heads down or I swear I'll give you what we used to call a reverse Mohawk myself." As Smith moved to go with them, Don grabbed his arm and yanked him back. "Not so fast. You're with me, Smith. Sit down on the table, right in front of the doorway."

Smith pulled out the chair the glowing woman had been sitting in. Don poked him with the weapon. "I said, *on* the table, not *at* it."

Smith obeyed, resting his feet on the seat of the chair. "Well?" he said stiffly.

Don backed up against the wall on the opposite side of the doorway from Judy and gave her a reassuring nod. "Just sit there, Smith. That's all bait is supposed to do."

Smith started to answer and then stopped. His eyes widened.

In the next moment, something tangled and ropy flew through the doorway past Don and Judy to land on Smith. The man tumbled over backwards with a high, wordless scream that actually chilled Don's blood, rolled sideways, and fell off the table onto the floor, struggling and gasping.

Don motioned for Judy to move back from the doorway and then looked at John. John half-rose, still aiming the weapon and started to yell, just as Don felt something cold, wet, and stringy slam into his torso and spread out to enfold him in a terrifyingly strong grip. The next thing he knew, he was on the floor, twisting, turning, bucking, trying to pull free of whatever it was. He had a glimpse of Will's and Penny's horrified faces and then he started to black out. Whatever it was was squeezing the breath out of him.

Far away in the gathering darkness, he heard Judy holler with surprise as she hit the floor. Why hadn't John fired? What was he waiting for?

Something was pulling at him, rolling him over so that he was face up now. The last thing he saw before he lost consciousness was the uniformed person standing over him. Must have been Will's Potty Police, he thought, spiraling down into darkness, because the person couldn't have been over ten years old.

"I seem to have made a mistake," a familiar voice was saying as John woke. A plain, somewhat dim ceiling swam into focus above him and he realized he was back in the transport they had first boarded with the alien. He raised his head. Yes, there it was, the blue-skinned, black-eyed creature who didn't know what a spacecraft was, even though it lived in one. It was sitting next to Maureen, who looked shell-shocked.

Then he remembered the bizarre things that had catapulted into the dining room and wrapped themselves first around Smith and Don and Judy, and then himself, when he had rushed to try to help Don. It had been like a cross between a net and a straightjacket, with the gripping power of an Oriental finger-trap — one of those basket-weave tube things that you put your fingers into at either end and then discover that the more you try to pull them out, the tighter the trap becomes. You had to push your fingers toward each other to loosen it up. The net-cum-straightjacket seemed to work on the same principle, with one important difference — it had felt like it was alive.

The thick ropy parts had had the squashy, repellent texture of a jellyfish; it had been throbbing, making it one of the most repellent things John Robinson could ever remember touching. He had rolled Don over to try to find some way to get him out of it and then those children had come in.

Rather, he had thought they were children. It was soon apparent to him that they were small and young-looking if not actually young, but most definitely not children. He had started to say something to the one standing over Don. She had raised her head, frowned at him as if he were distracting her with something unimportant and irrelevant, and then flicked a hand at him. He never saw the net until it was already on him, squeezing him into unconsciousness.

At least they let us live. We were going to shoot *them.*

Or *were* they going to let them live? He remembered the robot saying something about their going out the airlock and he sat up quickly, looking for Will and Penny.

Maureen was at his side immediately. "It's

okay, it's okay. We're all here, everybody's all right. The glowing ones call every way in and out of their area an airlock." She helped him up from the floor onto a seat. "We're being taken to another part of the — the city-world. World-city."

The glowing ones? World-city? He realized, with some disbelief, that he still had those damned headphones on. Damn, the things stuck as hard as an old-fashioned Hollywood stuntman's hat. He took them off and rubbed his painful ears. The alien said something that came to him as a continuous nasal whine, rising and falling in pitch, occasionally punctuated with something like a snore or a growl. Good thing it had handed out translating devices right away, he thought. God only knew how he would have reacted if he'd heard these sounds first.

"Our friend apologizes for the mistake," Maureen told him when he wouldn't put the earphones on again. "He . . . she . . . thought that we'd get along with the glowing ones."

"Great. So what do we do now?"

"Well, we're going to another part of the city. The glowing ones aren't the only inhabitants."

He skill felt a little dopey. "Who were those *children?*" he asked her.

Maureen stiffened a bit. "They weren't children —"

"I hope *not.*"

"— they're law enforcement. They don't glow, and they're kept small by some kind of inhibitor. The glowing ones use them for surveillance and protection. I'm not sure they're fully human, or the equivalent, because their brains are quite small. And they're sort of manufactured — our friend says the glowing ones grow them in vats."

"Who are the 'glowing ones?' And why were we sent to them?"

She insisted that he put on the headphones and then turned to the alien.

"The information we gathered from your world indicated food cycles and utilization of waste surplus was of utmost importance to you," the alien said, sounding neither apologetic nor embarrassed.

"Our worlds," John looked at Maureen. "Meaning the *Jupiter Two*?"

She nodded. "Where we were running low on food and high on waste."

"And then Smith asked to use the john."

"Which violated a serious taboo. You never mention excreting in the presence of food. It taints the entire room, makes everything unclean."

John looked at the alien again. "And it wasn't apparent that we didn't have the same kind of taboo?"

"It wasn't apparent that you didn't," the alien said mildly. "Your food and waste processes are meticulous. We thought the understanding was there."

"Who's 'we'?"

"We 'mystics.' Who 'live in the skin and contemplate the nothing.' " The alien chuckled.

"It's actually more complicated. We are those who . . ." It paused for so long that John thought it might have lost its train of thought. "Those who have the overview," it said at last. "Your life-partner has asked if there have been others who have come from other worlds. She has also tried to explain 'spacecraft' to me, but the closest I can get is 'traveling world.' "

John shook his head. "I don't understand. You obviously have the concept of transportation." He gestured at their surroundings.

"Yes, but no one *lives* in transportation," the alien said matter-of-factly. "And there is no point to transportation in the void because the void is the void. There is nowhere to go."

Before John could think of how to respond to that, Will spoke up. "And I've been trying to explain that it isn't so, Dad."

John forced himself to keep his voice neutral. "Have you."

Maureen cleared her throat. "When I woke up, Will was explaining the solar system. They never knocked him or Penny out."

He nodded unhappily. "I see."

"This view of the universe is truly *alien* to me," the alien said, unaware of how that sounded to them. "But in light of that, I find it easier to understand how you managed to inhabit your tiny world. The *Jupiter Two*," it corrected itself, with a glance at Will. "I think this other part of the city will be more hospitable for you. They will be more . . . open to new ideas. Especially the hyperdrive." The alien leaned forward. "They will want to know everything about your hyperdrive."

John stared at the alien, wondering what was really behind those unreadable eyes and that musical voice that sounded so unmusical without the headphones. "Yes, I'm sure they will."

Chapter Eight

His father wasn't terribly happy with him over this new development. The knowledge gave Will a sad sort of sour satisfaction. Neither he nor his father (nor anyone else for that matter) knew whether his telling the alien about space travel and the hyperdrive had been a good thing, a terrible mistake, or nothing to be concerned about either way, but he was pretty sure his father would be erring conservatively. Which was to say, his father was going to assume that Will had pulled one of the all-time mother-bloopers, if not the King Kong of dingdongs. Hell, maybe he really had.

Maybe, if he stopped to think about it, he'd come to the conclusion that he'd done one of the stupidest things a human being could do: telling some alien all about your home world and one of the latest scientific breakthroughs, which just happened to be built into your "traveling world." A race that didn't even believe in space flight not five minutes before you arrived suddenly gets not only a whole new picture of the universe, but also a working instrument to investigate it.

Will deliberately pushed away his trepidation. *Not now, thanks, I'm not being mad at my dad.*

Okay, so that was dumb, too. Everything he

did was dumb. Even the smart stuff turned out dumb. And who said he was really smart anyway? It had taken him an age and a half to rebuild the robot's brain, another dozen ages to figure out the arrangement of parallel processors and he skill couldn't keep the processors from overheating. Then aliens made contact with them by controlling his robot via their own remote power source, and followed that up by producing a duplicate within a couple of hours. He wanted to stop thinking about what they could do with the new information he'd given them. No doubt his father would turn out to be right.

And then a new thought struck him: *We never got to the planet where the gate was being built, and we never got back home. By the time the aliens find Earth —*

He felt as if he'd been punched. The Earth; the air and water running out; billions of people waiting for news of their safe arrival at the other hypergate, news that would never come.

What would happen to them now?

Or had it already happened?

The memory of his older self, image shimmering as the time gate closed between the *Jupiter Two* and the doomed planet they had crashed on, came to him. Those temporal fluctuations — when they had flown through the planet using the hyperdrive again, had they moved through time again as well?

There was no one to ask, no one who could

answer. Obviously, it was possible to change things — after all, he wasn't going to grow up orphaned and marooned alone with Dr. Smith. But you had to know what time it was, and there was no way anyone could figure that out —

His gaze fell on the robot and its twin, standing like a couple of dutiful sentries at the far end of the transport, side by side. If he could rig the robot to access the core log of the ship's computer, it might be able to determine if they had traveled in time as well as space during the final cataclysm when they had left the planet. If they had — well, he had managed to build a time gate with nothing more than *Jupiter Two* salvage in that future. He'd be able to do a lot more with the resources here. Even just the additional set of parallel processors would help a lot, he thought, looking at the duplicate, and not just with that. The extra processors could be the key to the conscious neural network he'd been chasing.

The thought of having more to work with than just what he could scrounge from the *Jupiter Two* spare parts sent him into sudden mental overdrive. He could practically see what he wanted to do, it was all right there in his head. All he needed were the parts, a surface to spread them out on, and some time to himself. And for the first time in a long time, he wasn't wishing for the impossible.

Maureen stopped at the threshold of the open

doorway and turned to the alien. “You don’t come into the city-world?”

“We live in the skin.” She sensed the equivalent of a smile in its voice. “The skin being the space between the outer barrier and the city. We are not suited for any other place.”

“There is a great deal I would like to ask you,” she said, feeling frustrated. John was waiting for her on the new arrival platform, along with everyone else. She ignored their impatience. “I want to know how you started living that way. I want to know how you live at all, where does your food come from, what is your culture —”

The dry, black eyes seemed to search her face for something. “Your small world was deceptive,” it said. “We thought your main concerns were ingesting and excreting efficiently, and indulging entertainments. You ask more questions than you would if that were true. And the news that there are many things in the void other than a scattering of worlds and some debris has been . . . disturbing. We must contemplate.” It took hold of her elbow and steered her over the threshold to the platform. “You must contemplate as well. If it is true that you have gone from surface world to little world to this world, you are way behind on your contemplation. You must now catch up, or risk —.”

Maureen started to say something else but the transport door closed in her face. She turned to John and spread her hands. He shrugged.

“Same city, different angle,” Penny said,

gazing out at the indoor cityscape. "I'm pretty sure, anyway. I didn't feel like we were going up or down. And the buildings all seem to be the same ones, though I can see some more that I couldn't before. I wonder what they're all for."

"What are all the buildings in Houston for?" Will asked her. "Or in any city?"

"Yeah, but this isn't a city like Houston," Penny said. "Or any other."

Maureen joined her younger daughter at the glass wall. It *was* like looking at any large, anonymous urban center, she thought; the similarities were striking enough to make you wonder. Then you'd realize you weren't sure what to wonder *about.*

Maybe you had to be very young to just accept it all at face value — that this was a logical arrangement for social life-forms, no matter where they originated, no matter what species. What about beehives and ant colonies, hornets and termites? Weren't those pretty much self-contained cities, after a fashion? An intelligent species made up of individuals, not a hive-mind, but faced with living in a hive structure — what else would it do but make a city out of it?

How many species, though? So far, they had met one black-eyed alien and one glowing human or humanoid. What else was waiting for them?

"This way," the robot said. It was standing in front of another open elevator with its double.

Maureen looked around at her family, at Don West, and at Smith.

"What else can we do?" she said.

"Maybe we'll find out," John said, and herded them into the elevator.

This time, however, it went down and then sideways for a fairly long time before it finally stopped and the doors opened on what reminded Maureen of a hospital room. More precisely, a surgical theater, except there were no operating tables, no instruments, and none of the usual surgery fittings. She put both arms out, to keep everyone from leaving the elevator. "Hello?" she asked. Her voice bounced off the tiled walls tankily. The behavior of sound waves was one of those universal constants, she thought; universal enough, anyway, to ensure that things like acoustics would be familiar to all species.

There was a radiolike crackle and a voice answered, "Hello," as if to confirm she had chosen the correct word. Don West moved up next to her, his weapon ready. He took a step out, putting only one foot over the threshold so that he straddled the room and the elevator, and looked around, the weapon following his gaze.

"Where are we now, please?" John asked, putting a hand on her shoulder.

"Immigration and job placement."

"Uh-huh." Don pulled his foot back inside the elevator and lowered the weapon, looking at John and Maureen. "At this point, I don't even know if that's strange anymore. I say we should find our way back to our friend with the weird eyes and the *Jupiter Two.* Just in case they decide they want to test out the new picture of the universe by going for a spin in our family camper."

"They won't," Judy said, the confidence in her tone raising Maureen's hackles for some silly reason. "They're too concerned about 'proximity madness,' remember? Besides, where would they get the fuel?"

Don ignored her. "Will, can you figure out how to operate this thing?"

"The robot can," said Will. "I'm just not sure it'll obey me."

"Then *ask* it, you little dunderhead," Smith snapped.

Everyone turned to look at him. Maureen saw that he was shifting his weight from one foot to the other, and his face seemed terribly pale, his lips nearly gray.

"Oh, that's right," Don said nastily. "Our friend Smitty here needs the little boys' room. Can't seem to hold it anymore, getting cranky?"

To Maureen's surprise, Smith only muttered something too low for anyone to hear and turned away. Even Don was nonplussed for a moment. Then he looked at Will, who faced the robot.

"Return us to our point of origin," he said.

The robot stood motionless while something inside went to work. *"Point of origin cannot be located."*

"I don't mean Earth. I mean, return this elevator to wherever it came from."

"Access denied," the robot said promptly.

"Please, come out."

They all turned toward the new voice, which came from the tiled room. Maureen blinked. For a moment, she was almost sure that she was looking at one of Penny's 3-D fashion videos from just before they had left. Body paint had come back in a big way, all over, one color, while the clothing designers had done another hark back to the mid-twentieth century again.

The dark green person standing alone in the middle of the room was not dressed in anything that recalled the mid-twentieth century on Earth, however. He — Maureen was reasonably sure that, in spite of the very long black hair, this was a male — was dressed in layers of various muted colors, wrapped or draped or tied. Even his shoes seemed to be made of wrapped cloth. Something shiny, a piece of metal, was stuck to the base of his throat. And like everyone else, he wore the translating headphones.

"Please come out," he said again. "There is no danger here."

"No offense," Don said, "but why should we trust you?"

"We trust you," the green man said, guilelessly.

Maureen felt herself on the verge of laughter. "That's the sort of logic that's so hard to argue with," she murmured.

"We want to be taken back to our ship," John

said, his voice firm, inviting no discussion. "The vehicle we arrived in."

"But would you not care to be out a little longer? Or are you all serving a penalty you must return for?"

Maureen looked at John. Suddenly, she felt awkward and foolish. "Are we going to give offense to everyone we meet here?"

John held her gaze a moment longer and then turned to Don West, who shrugged.

"Some of us are used to being the bull in the china shop," he said. "It comes with the job."

John frowned. "Right now, our best course of action might be to make friends instead."

Don West's expression was skeptical.

"Think about it," John went on. "Where are we going to go? And how would we get there?"

"Come out," urged the dark green man. His voice was gentle and almost pleading. "It's time to dismantle."

Don West put a hand on his weapon. "Dismantle *what?*"

"Your formation," the dark green man said. "You can now dismantle your formation."

Smith sighed noisily, holding his temples. "And the sooner the better."

Chapter Nine

Being dismantled, Zachary Smith reflected from deep within the haze of the Kiss, was the *only* way to live. Leave it to a society experienced in the pitfalls of permanent enclosure to understand group dynamics *and* the needs of the individual.

Especially the individual who needs to get high, eh, Zack?

Judy's parting shot to him, the last time he'd seen her. It still stung, although he also felt more philosophical about it. If she'd had to occupy his spot in the Robinson/*Jupiter Two* configuration, she would have needed to get high, too, make no mistake about *that.* But she hadn't had to, and she'd never have to, so she could perch on the highest point of her personal ivory tower and keep on looking down on doctors who used drugs.

If there was anything he hated, it was a sanctimonious medical practitioner. He'd always hated that kind, even back in med school. Prigs who'd never had to suffer any sort of privation, never known what it was like to wonder if you'd have enough money to stay in your apartment, or keep the power turned on, never had to make a deal with one of the many oily, smiling devils waiting around for poor students with a dream like medical school, something so far above them that actually gaining access would be nothing short of miraculous. Meanwhile, some of the most dismal examples of humanity, dolts whose knuckles didn't quite drag on the ground when they walked, who could have made that puerile, pea-brained pilot West look like an intellectual — *they* didn't have to worry, *they* were all the offspring of rich men and women. It didn't matter that the best education money could buy was completely wasted on them — what mattered was that they had the money to buy it.

Well, who was having the last laugh now but Zachary Smith, from the comfort and safety of this strange inside-out but most definitely livable world. And Earth could just go choke, he thought with lazy glee. If it hadn't already.

The golden haze that was his vision cleared a bit, enough for him to admire his surroundings. Nothing terribly luxurious by his old Earth standards, but for this world, definitely upper crust: a whole apartment, complete living quarters, entirely to himself.

Never mind that it was actually just one big room. It was one *big* room. Bigger than anything on the *Jupiter Two*, with the exception of the engine room and the bridge; bigger than the Robinsons' marital quarters. Sometimes, when he was in the peak of the Kiss, it seemed to be miles across. And all of it just for himself.

He planned to keep it that way, too. Oh, he might invite someone — Judy, for instance around for a bit of socializing, but that was all. He didn't ever want to have to live within ten feet of another intelligent creature ever again, if he could possibly help it.

Not like those fool Robinsons, anyway, Maw and Paw Robinson, insisting on being housed with the two youngest. He was surprised they could even stand being just with each other. Ah, the bourgeoisie, adhering to their useless conventions of behavior as if it really mattered to anyone *what* they did, as if there were some superior entity, or even a supreme being somewhere who was actually keeping score.

If there was, it was probably thinking that they were pretty stupid not to get dismantled when they'd had the chance.

Dismantled. Sometimes he thought it was about the funniest word he'd ever come across. Exactly why the translator had hit on *that* word, as opposed to something like . . . ah, but there his mind always seemed to draw a blank, even when he wasn't Kissed. It was a word that had certainly got their attention quickly enough. It didn't mean *killed, nullified,* or even *devalued. Taken apart:* that was all. And they had been, much to Smith's delight.

Dispersed was probably closer to the idea, except he doubted the worldview here could accommodate the real concept of dispersal. *Disbanded. Dissolved.*

Divorced.

What a relief *that* would be, he thought with a

laugh. A relief for everyone unlucky enough to have to endure the Robinsons stolidly doing that *family* thing that they did so well. He wouldn't be surprised to hear, sometime in the next few subjective months — they counted time differently here and he didn't have the hang of it yet — that Maw Robinson was having a baby. They'd probably name it John-Boy.

That *would* make everything just perfect, so perfect he wanted to vomit. Of course, it could have been a lot worse. John-Boy could have come along while they'd still been lost out there. He knew whom they'd have stuck with the baby-sitting.

The thought hit him funnier than he had expected. He started to laugh out loud and then couldn't stop.

Sometime later, he found himself half off the futon-style bed, staring up at the patterns on the ceiling as he got his breath back. He had decided that the patterns were really there. Then he remembered proving it, climbing up on the desk between the end of one dose and the beginning of another, and touching the ridges with his fingertips, just because he wanted to know. Under any other circumstances, he would have thought that a stupid and silly thing to do; now he was finding new appreciation for having such luxuries as being able to do something stupid and silly rather than economical and to some practical point.

Not that he was going to stay high forever, no

matter what Dr. Sanctimonious Judy Robinson thought. But after being a genuine prisoner aboard that damned *Jupiter Two* — the only one who wasn't there voluntarily — he needed to cut loose, blow out, go over the top. Thank God he could finally be allowed to do it undisturbed.

And with as much raw material for the Kiss as he could have wished for, obligingly supplied by their new friends. *His* new friends — he doubted they were interested in getting acquainted with Judy or any of the rest of her saintly family. His new friends who had an appreciation for intoxicants, a willingness to learn about new ones, and, if he remembered rightly, a few ideas about how to work it into the system profitably. They were coming around to talk to him about it sometime soon, too, he remembered, although he couldn't bring to mind exactly when.

There was a bell-like clanging sound somewhere nearby. It took him a moment to remember that this must be the thing they used for a doorbell around here, a piece of rounded metal with a small rod hanging off it by a bit of rope. You hit the metal with the rod, kind of gong-style. No generated energy wasted just to announce you'd come to visit; one of the rules that Smith found amazingly practical and sensible. If sanctimonious.

Regardless, it had to be his new circle of friends at the door, ready to come in and talk about terms of this and that. Pity he didn't have an agent, he thought. Give it time. Before long, he'd have everything he could possibly want and a few more things he hadn't thought of wanting. Such were the perks of getting in on the rock-bottom ground floor of a new industry. Hell, he thought, pushing himself up from the couch and crossing the broad room to the door, he might even get to control the slang and get everyone to call him Dr. Feelgood instead of a dealer or a pusher —

He stood with the door open, staring, unable to think of anything to say.

"What's the matter, Zach," said Judy. "Can't you remember my name anymore? Or is the face drawing just as much of a blank for you now, too?"

"Judith," he said finally. "You — What do you want?"

She walked in, pushing him aside gently with one hand, and looked around. "Got yourself a nice big room, I see. Or is it just the fact that there's almost no furniture that makes it just look enormous?"

He blinked at her helplessly.

"Or can't you decide?" She strolled over to him, her arms folded across her front. She was wearing one of the native wrapped-cloth outfits in a rich forest green that made her hair look like spun gold. It was loose around her shoulders now rather than pulled back efficiently, the way she usually wore it, and he saw the glint of earrings. He had always wondered what kind of jewelry she would like.

"What *do* you want?" he asked her again after a moment, gazing into her face with curiosity.

"I keep asking myself the same question, actually," she said irritably. "I keep telling myself it's none of my business, that if things hadn't gone wrong for *you*, you'd be enjoying an early and affluent retirement somewhere and I'd be nothing. Literally. You didn't give that a second thought, so why *I* should care about what happens to you is quite, quite beyond me. Except perhaps as a professional." Her large eyes stared hard; he was too stoned to look away "Perhaps it's the same thing that made me become a doctor in the first place."

Smith shook his head, bewildered.

"Did you understand a single word I just said?" Judy asked him.

"Well . . . no." He was also too stoned to lie.

"Didn't think so." She paused. "I have a mezzanine room in one of the medical buildings. It includes laboratory privileges, and the lab is nothing to sneeze at. You should pardon the expression."

He waited for her to get to the point. Somewhere deep in his brain, the fog was trying to disperse and he was doing his best to keep it dense, dark, and impenetrable.

She blew out an impatient breath. "I happen to know there are a few vacancies. There's room in one of the labs, too, for anyone interested in research. Their work in immunology and longevity is —" she stopped and looked at him with narrowed eyes. “Hello? Are you getting this?”

He closed his eyes briefly. “Immunology and longevity. So?”

She nodded. “So you’d rather waste your intellect, your training, and what’s left of your life like this. Am I right?”

What he wanted to say was, *You’ve absolutely ruined my high with your pious prattle.* But it wouldn’t come. Perhaps because he knew it would be wasted on her — what did she know about needing anesthesia, or even an analgesic? She’d never been in pain in her life. She’d caused plenty, but had experienced none.

“Oh, for crying out loud,” she said in disgust. “You can’t even tell me to go to hell, can you? The big saboteur, the terrorist *manqué*. You can’t even get up on your hind legs and fight like a human. Because you’d rather be high.”

He shrugged, wondering what she wanted him to say to something like that. Apparently, she was one of those unfortunates who thought she was stimulating argument and discussion when she was actually cutting off all chance of response.

“Fine. Do anything you want. You always have, unless forcibly restrained. Isn’t that right? Sure. But at least I can say that I tried.” She turned away from him and headed for the door. Smith stared after her, feeling a recondite mix of relief and sorrow that she was going. She waited in the open doorway for a moment, gazing at him. “I guess I’m a fool, but the offer stays open.

Any time you feel like you want to sober up and live for real, code me." She jerked her chin at the comm unit in the wall, which functioned both as a sort of telephone and e-mail system. She hesitated. "I'd say something like, 'You know how to code, don't you? You just get up your nerve and go.' Except I think the reference would be wasted on you. Just like my concern."

" 'You just put your lips together and blow.' " He blurted it out more than anything, before he could even stop to think. But to his satisfaction, he saw that he had surprised her. He could also see that he had managed to render her speechless. She couldn't think of a single smart-ass retort before she slipped out, closing the door firmly behind her.

At this point, he knew that a whistle à la Bogart would have been the height of wit, even with no one else to hear it. But the pitiful truth was that Zachary Smith was one of those people who really and truly could not whistle. Not even if his life had depended on it.

Chapter Ten

And this, John Robinson thought a bit nervously, is the part where we could decide to live happily ever after.

He sat alone on a bench in what they might have called a sculpture gallery back on Earth. Except on Earth, it probably would have been a sculpture *garden,* in an arboretum. Never mind. Earth would seem to have become a dead issue. Or, rather, *closed* issue, to put it a little less morbidly.

Maybe it would be easier for Will and Penny, he thought, as a pair of young people in the local, scaled-down version of shepherd chic passed him. He recognized that they were in conversation, although most of it was an odd combination of semaphore and body language, nothing spoken. Not that he would have understood anything if they had been speaking aloud; his earphones were back in the apartment that the locals had allocated to him and Maureen.

He could not have said why he'd chosen to venture out incommunicado. It was the kind of passive-aggressive rudeness he most despised — at its best, that was. Short of vandalism or theft, it was probably about as antisocial an act as you could commit in this place to go without a translating device. Of course, the citizens here had dispensed with clumsy headphones. According to their sponsor (at least, he thought *sponsor* was the general idea), Inrica, a small implant just under the skin behind either ear took care of everyone's translating needs. John had wanted to ask exactly how much anyone needed a translator, but somehow the conversation shifted out from under him. Or maybe his headphones had chosen that moment to short out and he hadn't understood.

But then, as Maureen had pointed out when they'd been alone later, maybe they were missing an awful lot even with headphones.

Alone. With Maureen. For the first time in who knew how long, they had been really alone together. Their apartment included living space for Penny and Will and, at John's insistence, Don West, who hadn't argued.

Now Will and Penny had taken Inrica's offer of an orientation tour and rushed out quickly enough to leave a hole in the air. Don had followed immediately, looking a silent promise at him and Maureen that the kids would come to no harm.

In the suddenly empty apartment he and Maureen had simply stood looking at each other as if they'd been stunned, too stunned to believe they were no longer on the *Jupiter Two.*

"What happens now?" he'd said finally, after some unmeasureable eternity. And it seemed to take another eternity for her to answer.

"I wanted to say something like, 'How quickly

they forget,' or 'Don't worry, it's just like riding a bike,' but witty repartee is appropriate only when you actually have the answers." Her expression wavered between defiance and vulnerability and he was pretty sure that it mirrored his own. "I'm shell-shocked." She started to turn away from him.

He caught her arm. "I know. I am, too. It's really true, what the old song says, about how you never know what you have till it's gone."

She stared at him warily. "Oh?"

"Yeah. In this case, certainty."

Her eyes widened. "How do you mean?"

"Personally, I never realized how much in my life was certain. Things I knew for sure would happen, all day, everyday. I knew so much about how my life would go, what was going to happen that I'd all but forgotten most of it." He gave a short laugh. "I can remember my father talking about some hotshot prodigy they'd brought in one time as a strategist. Just a kid, not even sixteen, but a brain the size of a continent. I remember him telling my mother that the kid really was brilliant, but it was all intellectual. He had no real experience in any context. And my father said, 'What I've forgotten about battle strategy it'll take this kid the rest of his life to learn.' And that's what I feel like right now. What I've forgotten about how to live on Earth, it'll take me the rest of my life to learn again here."

Then they were in each other's arms, clinging

to each other, touching, holding, as if letting go would mean they'd both fall down some long, dark abyss. After that, it was like a reaffirmation of their humanity, their status as humans, and then humans committed to each other. The return of a few particular certainties, the only ones that humans ever really owned, and could give each other.

It made a difference. Afterwards, they lay on the futonlike pad, still holding tight to each other, but there was no longer any desperation between them. "I'll be your life jacket," Maureen had said, "if you'll be mine."

He'd kissed her on the forehead. "It's a deal."

At the moment, his life jacket was trying to hunt up information on food production and he had a feeling she wasn't having much luck. She had no reason, as far as the inhabitants here were concerned, to know anything about food production. And in his own opinion, it wasn't an issue worth bothering with. The food in this part of the world wasn't interesting enough to be described even as dull. Processed nutrition, molded into things like crackers and bread rolls, and formulated to prevent any possibility of stomach upset or heartburn — it occurred to him you'd have a hard time indulging in food for enjoyment, or as an enhancement to a social function. And then again, he thought, one of humanity's least attractive features had been the ease with which one part of it indulged itself to death while the rest of it died of hunger and thirst. So perhaps they had the right idea here after all.

In time, all of their questions as to how the world worked would answered, Inrica had told them. John couldn't get over the idea that the compact young man who appeared to be around Don West's age but wasn't much taller than Will found them laughable in their ignorance. The interstellar equivalent of yokels or hillbillies, maybe. Their story of living on the surface of their world was met with polite skepticism, as if they were a group of barbarians who had sailed in from some uncharted island in the middle of the ocean and were convinced they had sailed off the edge of the flat Earth.

But at least the skepticism was polite rather than scornful or contemptuous. It crossed his mind that etiquette was probably more than half the reason this place had lasted as long as it had. However long that might have been — they kept brushing aside all his questions about clock and calendar measurements, claiming it couldn't possibly make sense to him. Still, there were signs that this was a long-lived civilization, even if not exactly ancient enough for fossils. They had managed not only to survive in their limited space but to develop. (Evolve, too, maybe? He'd have to ask Maureen and Judy.) So they must have been doing something right, something they were still doing.

Suddenly he imagined himself returning to

Earth from their long wander among the stars, and talking about this at length. What a press conference that would be (assuming such things as press conferences still existed). *Dateline, Houston: Space Castaways Reveal Secret for the Survival of the Species: 'Please' and 'Thank you.'* And on Earth, if it was still there and still the world they knew, the skepticism meeting that statement wouldn't be anywhere near polite. Thus demonstrating conclusively that Earth had indeed missed the point.

Might as well not bother trying to get back, if you already know what's going to happen.

The thought reverberated in his mind and he understood that he had not relinquished the hope of seeing Earth again. Had not . . . and would not.

Will looked around the room, the size of the auditorium at his old school back in Houston, where it seemed like something akin to a computer-science fair was in progress. Except the multicolored participants were mostly Judy's age, with a few older people, and no kids at all. They all had their own work areas, each tailored to the user's preferences — some were long tables while others utilized an arrangement of shelves and pull-out surfaces, and one woman had a whole bunch of stuff just spread out on a drop cloth on the floor. A few people were working strictly with holograms, no physical tools or components, and he wondered how they could actually get any results. It took him a while to realize that the holograms were projections of certain works-in-progress elsewhere in the room.

He turned to Inrica, who gave him an encouraging nod. "This is what you would call our artificial intelligence project."

"Cool," Will said, looking around again. "How's it going."

Inrica pointed at a vacant workspace. No, not quite vacant — the robot and its twin were both there, side by side as if they'd been waiting patiently for him to show up. They were surrounded on three sides by a set of workbench modules exactly the way he liked them. "We thought you might see for yourself."

Now he knew just what Penny meant when she said her heart leaped. Will started toward the workspace and then hesitated.

"Something wrong?" Inrica asked him in that friendly, I'll-be-your-host voice.

Will turned back to him slowly, trying to think how to word his next question so as not to offend and get himself and everyone else into trouble.

"Why are you giving me all this?" he said finally.

"Giving you all what?" Inrica's midnight-blue face was honestly puzzled.

Will gestured at the workspace.

The man's confusion deepened. "Are we wrong? Is this *not* work that you are interested in?"

"No, it's not that," Will said, wincing. "I just

don't understand why you're giving me all this. Just handing it to me." He paused. "I mean, do you guys just *give* stuff away to anyone who wants it?"

The question only seemed to confuse Inrica even more. "As your own artificial intelligence project might say, 'That does not compute.' "

"You mean, it doesn't make sense?"

"No."

"But —" Will floundered. There was some fundamental assumption at the basis of everything that he and Inrica didn't share — he could grasp that much from the logic classes he'd had. But he didn't have enough information yet to understand what that assumption was.

"In your little world," Inrica said suddenly, "you and your family — did you give each other anything?"

Will blinked at him. "Like what?"

"Work. Food. A place to sleep."

"Well . . . of course. I mean — not exactly. We all — we were the crew. We were family *and* the crew at the same time. We agreed. Well, *kinda.* I mean, this was the mission. We all knew what we had to do —" Will blew out a breath. "I don't think I can explain this real well. You ought to talk to my mother and father. Or maybe Major West. He's not really part of the family — well, he wasn't, but because of the way the mission is, he sort of is now. I mean, for us, it's like there's not really any difference between family and crew . . ." he trailed off as a glimmer of understanding finally came to him.

"It's very much the same here," Inrica told him. "It has to be. Our life-space is rigidly defined and bounded. We all know what we have to do. Each of us wants to do what we have to do. What you describe as your 'mission,' we call a way of life."

"I don't think that's quite right," Will said, "but I can't figure out where it's off." He thought for a moment longer. "How do you manage to get everyone to want to do what they have to?"

Inrica looked puzzled again. "How did *you?*"

"You mean on the *Jupiter Two*?" Will shrugged. "We just did. It's the way we are."

"So there's your answer." Inrica led him over to his new workplace. "Now, you make an inventory of things you have and things you need —"

"I just have one more question," Will told him, forcing him to stop.

Inrica nodded patiently. That was one thing in this place's favor, Will thought, the way most of the people here seemed to be so patient. Unless they glowed, apparently.

"What do you do with people who *don't* want to do what you tell them they have to?"

"But why would they have to be told in the first place?" Inrica asked.

"How else are they gonna know?"

Inrica shook his head. "Did *you* have to be *told* to be interested in artificial intelligence?"

"No. I just was. But I didn't know I would be

until I learned about it."

"So you learned," Inrica said happily, as if that settled everything, and turned to go.

"No, *wait.*" Will was starting to feel a little desperate. "What do you do about someone who learns about something and they're *not* interested. Like, you have someone who learns about this — artificial intelligence, say — but they don't want to do it. I mean — it's like you need them to do something and they're not interested?"

Inrica looked from far on his left all the way to his right, a mannerism Will recognized as the local version of a shrug. "I don't know. We've never had anyone like that here."

Will stared after him as he walked away, too startled to call him back and ask him to explain *that* bit of information. Just as well — he had a feeling that whatever the explanation was, he wasn't going to like it.

He leaned on one of the workbenches, wishing he hadn't been so eager to get away from everyone else. Most of all, he wished Penny could have heard all this before they'd let her off at the place with all the artists. If those people *were* artists.

And if *artist* meant the same thing here that it did back home . . .

"Oh boy," he muttered.

On the other side of the workbench, the robot — his own robot — suddenly came to life. "*Vocal pattern indicates the development of a problem or problems,"* it said. *"Robot detects no systemic or mechanical malfunction."*

Chin on his fists, Will gazed at it thoughtfully. "Maybe I can fix that."

Chapter Eleven

" 'Glowing' people?" The pale-green man and his two pale-green companions didn't look at each other, but Zachary Smith couldn't get over the feeling that *something* had passed between each one of them in some other way. Or maybe the combination of early-stage withdrawal combined with culture shock was tuning him to the paranoia channel. So to speak. Who *had* spoken that way, anyhow? One of his old classmates, or someone from the Houston med —

"What 'glowing people'?" the pale-green man asked, and Smith realized it was the second time he'd said it. He struggled to get his mind back on track. Another side effect of this stupid withdrawal was an inability to concentrate and a twentieth-century attention span.

"When we first came here, whoever — *whatever* — met us and gave us these translating devices took us to a place where we ate a meal with a glowing woman," Smith said, trying to watch all their expressions at once. A remark West had made about not wanting to play poker with these people crossed his mind. "I — We offended her and so we were brought here —"

"*All* of you had this experience?" the pale-green man said with some surprise.

"Why do you ask?"

"I've never heard of so many having the same entry experience simultaneously." He turned to the woman sitting on his right in a pear-shaped chair hanging on a flexible rope that dangled from a simple crossbar arrangement. It looked just like the one that that miserable wretch West had forced everyone (except him) to do chin-ups on, Smith thought. "Have you?"

"Two people, maybe three. Never as many as seven. Her strange, light-colored pupils suddenly made him think of miniature flashlights "But it could have been a special case. That pigmentation says as much."

Smith looked down at his hands and then up at her, feeling mildly uneasy. "Are you saying you have some problem with my *color?*"

The woman leaned forward slightly, her squarish face filled with disbelief. "What would make you ask a question like *that?*"

"Where I come from, it was often an issue."

The woman sitting on the man's other side made a scornful noise. "Send him back to his nest, Javven." she said. "Obviously, someone's made a grievous predecanting error."

"Maybe not," the man said. "It could be an experiment. We do have our adherents and believers in that area. Once in a while, when they think it's absolutely safe to slip in something, try something new —" he paused, looking from one woman to the other. "Wouldn't a visionary be mistaken for a madman?"

"And a madman mistakes himself for a visionary," said the second woman. "So who's right?"

"Oh, I do have a vision," Smith put in before they could start arguing with each other. "But it's a very practical kind of vision."

"A practical vision," the same woman said. "I wouldn't mind having one of those. Not that the other kind isn't entertaining."

"I'm glad you enjoyed it," Smith purred at her. "But the sort of vision I was referring to is *about* our product, rather than produced *by* it."

She glanced at the man to her right and then smiled back at him.

"I see a world of happy people," Smith said expansively. "I see a world filled with people who are no strangers to pleasure, who let nothing come between them and anything they enjoy. And I see us — you three, and I — as the facilitators of this b-bright n-n-new order." He took a breath. He'd nearly said *brave new world,* of all the damned things.

"The four of us to start with," the man said. "What you have to understand is that there are more than four of us."

Smith frowned, imagining the Incredible Shrinking Profit. "How many more?"

"Not enough for an army, or even a good-sized mob," the man said with a smile. "And they're all spread out, through the various areas in the city. But their faith is strong."

"Faith," Smith echoed. *Oh no. Not a weird religious cult* — "Faith in what?"

The man leaned toward him confidentially. "We believe that the great nothing we float in actually contains not just this place where we live, but many, many realms — worlds. Worlds that, in some cases, contain intelligent life."

Smith hoped his face was as frozen as he was trying to make it.

"Intelligent life that may well have visited us," the man went on suddenly. "That may be walking among us even now."

"Oh." Smith wet his lips. "I see."

"Not all of us go *that* far," said the first woman quickly. "I mean, I'll grant you the existence of other worlds, but alien visitation? Somehow, I don't think it's possible it could have happened without anyone knowing."

Smith resisted the urge to clap his hands together and rub them vigorously. God in heaven, it was true, not only on Earth but everywhere — a mark born every minute, and two to take him. But if you were *really* lucky, you wouldn't have to split with anyone.

"It seems I have some interesting news for you," he said.

"Your friend has come after all."

Judy looked up from the screen that jutted out from the desk. It was the teak-colored woman named Pir, who had given her access to the longevity studies. Computer language here was incomprehensible to her but the general operating interface had been made for idiots. Thank God

— the wealth of information they had was astoundingly full and detailed. She still hadn't figured out how to translate their time measurement into something she could understand, so she didn't know how long it had taken for them to acquire so much data. It seemed to have been compiled in a shorter period of time than would have been possible on Earth. A deep cultural commitment to the search for knowledge, perhaps? If so, she had arrived in heaven without the bother of dying.

For this reason alone, she would have been annoyed at being interrupted, except that she had told the helpful and intelligent Pir about Smith (in a very abbreviated way). She turned around, hoping he was here because she'd actually gotten through to him —

The smile on her face faded, giving way to an expression of puzzlement.

"Gee, thanks, Doc," Don West said. "You really got a way of making a guy feel welcome. If only you had a cup of water. Then we could have another perfect moment together."

Judy looked at Pir a bit ruefully. "This isn't the one I was telling you about."

Pir looked from her to Don West and back again. "So much the better. Nobody has only *one* friend." She went back to her own workspace, which was mostly tanks of biological matter that required a great deal of temperature measurement.

"OK, I can guess you thought I was someone

else," he said, coming closer, "but I confess I'm stumped as to who. Were you expecting an old friend or a new friend?"

"Just a colleague," she said briskly and smiled at him. "What's up, Major? Besides your hackles, I mean?"

"My radar." He half-sat on the desk and folded his arms. "Or are you not familiar with that old term?"

"It's still good enough for the bats," she said, "so, yes, I'm well acquainted with radar. What's on yours?"

"Easier to tell you what isn't."

"All right." She mirrored his position at the other end of the desk. "What's *not* on your radar, then?"

His annoyance deepened. "Jesus, what *is* it with you Robinsons? You get a comfortable bed and three squares and you think all's well that ends well?"

She kept a pleasant expression fixed on her face. "It doesn't always pay to go around *looking* as suspicious as you might feel, Major. You won't make any friends that way, and if you don't have friends, you can't find out very much, can you?"

She saw him relax just the tiniest bit. "All right. You had me going there for a while. I thought you were all going native."

"But when you think about it, Don, what choice do we really have? Where else are we going to go but native?"

His posture stiffened again. "I thought you were a lot smarter than to take all this on face value. Me, I'm nowhere near as smart as you. On the Doc Judy graph of smart, I bet I don't even raise so much as a blip. But one thing I *do* know is that there's a hell of a lot I *don't* know. And that's the problem with being as smart as you — it's too easy for you to think you know more than you really do. That's the kind of mistake that can kill you. For real."

"I'm trying to learn," Judy said, unable to keep the impatience out of her voice. "What's *your* excuse?"

"I don't make excuses. I wanted to talk over some stuff that's bothering me with someone. I think your parents are a little busy, I'd just scare Will and Penny, and I'd kill Smith. You're elected." He paused. "Try not to turn handsprings with joy, you'll just embarrass me."

Her smile became sly. "Who told you about my gymnast period? Never mind. Of course you can talk to me, Major. Don. Really." She sobered under his gaze, starting to feel ashamed of herself for treating him so flippantly when he had come to her with something serious to discuss.

He opened his mouth and then hesitated, looking around. "You mind if we go someplace else?"

There were only a couple of other people in the room besides Pir and themselves, a slightly older man named Wann, or possibly Juan, and a woman who seemed to be in long-term attachment to an optical gadget that Judy took to be the local version of an electron microscope. "No one'll bother us, if that's what you're concerned about."

Don shrugged. "Let's say I think better when I'm moving. You know what Satchel Paige said about jangling around loosely to keep yourself limber."

"He also said not to look back because something might be gaining on you." She reached over and blanked the computer screen. "All right, then. Let's go for a walk. I won't look back if you won't."

On Earth, the wide, round, intricately carved pedestal would have been spouting water rather than colored light. The light patterns, like the carving on the object they issued from, were all abstract but hinting at a certain logic that Judy wasn't sure she would ever decipher. Nonetheless, she found it entertaining, or at least novel.

"You have to admit," she said, leaning forward on the bench, "they really know how to do a park here."

"You think this is a park?" Don touched the bench with one finger, as if he weren't sure that it was going to remain solid. "I can't get my mind around that one. It's indoors. Everything's indoors, here. Feels *weird.*"

"Well, of course it does," she said. "But that'd be like going to our planet and complaining that everything's located within the atmosphere, where there's always light and air. Sort of air. Anyway, come on — you and I have spent just about all our lives in comfort domes before now. Being indoors all the time is old news."

"But we knew the difference."

Judy sighed impatiently. "They *do* have boundaries here. Home, private space, public space, common space." She gestured at the light fountain. "OK, don't call it a park, call it a comfort dome, call it a mall, call it madam."

"I'm saying we knew the difference. *Know* the difference." He paused as two men passed, although neither of them glanced in their direction. "These people think there's this, and there's void, and that's all."

"And I seem to remember you saying when we got pulled into that opening that they'd done this before," Judy said. "You want to explain that?"

"I *can't*," Don said, keeping his voice low. "We got sucked in here like this was spaceport central and then everybody we meet insists they don't believe in outer space or UFOs or life on other planets. Especially the *on* part. So assuming the weirdo with the weirdo eyes is basically just a greeter, then who the hell built that opening, who ran that tractor beam, and where are they now?"

Judy wet her lips. "Well . . . maybe it's all just automatic now, whenever something like the *Jupiter Two* comes in range of it. Maybe whoever used to run it died off and the rest of them forgot about it."

"Uh-huh," Don stood up and turned around, putting one foot on the bench and leaning his arms on his bent knee. Watching their backs Judy realized. She looked over her shoulder but didn't see anything gaining on them. There was only one of many passages that led off the park area where they were sitting like so many spokes on a wheel. It was as wide as any city street in Houston and ran between two rows of structures, some of which were completely transparent, revealing rooms that were quite recognizable as gymnasiums, classrooms, offices, and production studios, as well as other laboratories. She'd wondered what the rationale was behind making some places transparent and others not, but there seemed to be no clear-cut plan. Maybe it was just another of those cultural things, possibly even just an architect's decision. Back in the twentieth century, her grandmother had told her, a mere architectural design had ended up dictating a whole slew of open-plan elementary schools in the U.S., with no walls to divide one class of kids from another. According to Grandma, this had caused everything from inability to concentrate among students to chronic nervous breakdowns among teachers. But then Grandma had never been progressive about educational systems.

So what kind of disorders would transparent buildings engender, she wondered, and made a mental note to look into whatever translated as psychiatry here.

"Now that you've got that figured," Don said, making her jump, "explain to me why there are no animals here, and no children." He looked down into her startled face. "Or hadn't you noticed about the children?"

"I — I'm not sure," she admitted. "I wasn't thinking about that. To be honest, I'm kind of surprised that you are."

"Anyone who's seen any combat thinks about children," Don said. "Oh, I remember that famous those-who-can't-think-fight quote. I can even remember who it was that said it. So if you ever happen to be caught in a refugee camp between two feuding warlords, tell me who you want walking the perimeter for you — someone who thinks or someone who fights?"

He paused, but she doubted that he was really expecting an answer from her. "Last duty I pulled before I qualified for space was airlifting the Mandela Republic orphans," he went on after a moment. "I wasn't quite sixteen years old and I wished to God that I *coulda* stopped thinking after that one."

She reached up and put a hand on his arm. He didn't acknowledge her touch, but he didn't pull away.

"And don't give me a lot of compassion-speak about how I was just a kid myself. By the time I was sixteen, I hadn't been a kid for a long, long time. But *they* were kids, those orphans. Hell, they were *babies*. Toddlers, little tykes. They should have been running around in playgrounds under the sun, they —" He took a breath. "I'm not trying to make you feel sorry or shed a tear for the old vet, I'm really not." Finally he turned to look directly at her. "I just want you to know that when you write me off as some kind of dumb muscle-head flyboy with a short fuse, you do me as much a disservice as me calling you 'babe.' If you get my meaning here."

She left her hand on his arm. "Point taken, Major West. I'll try not to step on your toes in the future."

"Especially in high heels, OK?" He winked at her and she laughed. "But getting back to the situation at hand, there are no kids here. *None.* Unless they're hiding them real, real good. And if they are — *why?*" He gestured at the nearest transparent building, an office building that seemed to have been partially modeled, at least externally, on an airplane hangar.

"Maybe they send them away to creche-type places or what we'd call boarding schools for their education," Judy said, wincing at how lame that sounded even to herself.

"It might be that specialized in parts of a city, but everywhere?" He looked around. "The nearest thing we saw to a kid was those law enforcement creatures, and the resemblance was only physical. And they weren't animals, either."

"It was probably hard to keep animals alive in a completely interior world," Judy suggested. "The myth that glowing woman told us indicates they must have lived on the surface of some planet in the distant past. They very well could have gone underground here after some major cataclysm that wiped out their homeworld. Think of Earth. We barely have any animals left ourselves. Had any, I mean."

"Yeah, your guess is as good as mine." He moved around to her other side and stood gazing at the skyline on the other side of the fountain. Skyline? Building-line? City-line? Terminology went wonky in a situation like this. "All right. Let's say that the kids are all away at boarding school and all the animals are extinct. Where does that leave the old people?"

"I've seen lots of older people," she said uncomfortably.

"Older, sure. But not *old."*

"If you'd seen all their research on longevity, you'd hesitate before you assumed how old anyone here is, or isn't."

"You don't sound too sure about that, Doc." He looked at her again. "You sure you're looking at real data, stuff they've done? Or is it all theoretical? How is it presented?"

"Mostly events recorded in real-time video, with narration. All their archives translate into spoken word. They don't seem to write anything down, except maybe pictures."

"Icons, perhaps."

"Icons?"

"Just thinking out loud. Why do you suppose there's no writing?"

Judy floundered. "They got out of the habit,

what with all the video recording?"

"Maybe all their pens ran out of ink and they didn't have any squid to refill them. How the hell does *writing* die out in a civilization as advanced as this one?"

"I don't *know,*" she said, spooked and unhappy. "I just *don't know.*"

"I didn't expect you to." He moved quickly to sit down next to her, slipping an arm around her shoulders. "And I'm not trying to scare you. But I had to get you thinking. I know we've got nowhere else to go, and no way to get there even if we did. But that's not the signal to lay down and die. We survived this long, why break the habit?"

She realized she'd been holding her breath and let it out in a long sigh. "OK. But let me ask you a few now." She pulled away slightly and started ticking her questions off on her fingers. "Why do you assume we're in danger of lying down and dying? Did you ever think of asking the locals some of those questions, about kids and old people? And when you decided to come riding in on your white horse to rescue my brain and get me thinking, did it occur to you that you might just be making it damn near impossible for me to continue behaving normally so that I *can* find things out?"

"Well, Secret Agent Robinson, pull yourself together. Sometimes you gotta go from zero to sixty and back again in the space of two seconds — that's just how it is in the danger zone and being lost in space definitely qualifies as being in the danger zone." He folded his arms again and crossed his left ankle over his right knee. "As for your first two questions, its like this: Number one, I'm not *assuming,* I'm looking out for your spoiled Robinson butt. Walking the perimeter. And number two, it's gonna sound real strange for someone like me to ask the local civilians about kids and old people. But you're a doctor. Maybe they already think it's pretty strange that you haven't asked."

"Penny and Will —"

He nodded. "You know where they are?"

"Are they — Did they —" she felt panic rising, starting to choke her.

"Relax, relax. *I* know where they are. You and your parents can thank me later. I followed our host when he took them out. Penny's in some kind of artsy-fartsy joint and Will's building robots or something."

Laughter poured out of her in a relief that bordered on hysteria but didn't cross over. Fortunate — she didn't want to give him any more ammunition in the way of things like her spoiled Robinson butt. So-called. Some tiny, distant part of her had already vowed to get him for that one. If they were all ever safe enough again, she would, too. She would.

"Aren't you the detective," she said breathlessly after a while. "Oh, I'm not making fun of you, Don, and I'm not making light of anything. I'm surprised my parents actually let them out of their sight."

"Well, I did tell them I'd tag along discreetly and make sure nothing happened to —"

She gave him a hard shove. "Oh, you *bastard.*"

"What?" he said, putting his hands up defensively.

"You had me thinking my parents just let Penny and Will walk off without a second thought." She slapped at his hands and forearms. "That was a really *lousy* thing to do, you *scum,* you *muscle-headed flyboy with a short fuse* —"

"Hey, look who's talking short fuse here!" In a moment, he had her arms pinned behind her back.

Oh boy, she thought, staring up into his eyes. She was close enough to see her own reflection in them, and to see the fine worry lines between his eyebrows. *Could it get any more cliché than this?*

His head seemed about to dip and then he suddenly let go of her and sat back. She found herself blinking in amazement.

"Oh, come on, Doc," he said and actually chucked her under the chin. "You don't *really* think I'm such a walking cliché, do you?"

"You *bastard!*" she shrieked at him and, laughing, started hitting him again.

He jumped up and backed away from her, also laughing. "Uh-uh, Doc. Tell you what — suppose *you* pin *me* next time?"

She rose and cocked a fist at him, unsure of just how playful she really felt. *"You b—"*

"Hey, who was it who said those who can't

think, fight?" He threw her a salute and left, going back the way they had come. She waited until he had disappeared before heading back to her work at the laboratory.

Chapter Twelve

Okay, Don West thought, gazing up and down the clean, building-lined boulevard, *never mind the kids and the old people — where's the damned* traffic?

As if in answer to his question, one of the small vehicles that served as public transportation hummed past him, hovering maglev-style above a shiny stripe in the pavement that seemed to be inert otherwise. He stepped back so it wouldn't slow down for him and watched it cruise away on its endless journey through the city. He laughed to himself. Whatever you wanted to call those things — robo-taxis, microbuses, model trains (there were two-, four-, and six-seaters), it sure as hell wasn't traffic. This city had no traffic whatsoever — just lots of pedestrians and those automated go-carts. He made a mental note to hunt up their source and then had a sudden vision of them being grown in vats with child-sized android storm troopers.

The idea made him queasy. Of course, if he was foolish enough to repeat it to Maureen when he found her, she'd tell him what nonsense it was in the plainest terms possible.

Wouldn't she?

Sure. And what would she tell him about the absence of children and old people?

"When school was in session in Houston, Major, you could go all day, from eight in the morning till after four, without seeing a single person under the age of eighteen." Maureen Robinson stood watching as a team of six people, each in an individual mobile that could have been a cherry picker except for the impossibly long, graceful legs on each unit, worked carefully at removing a layer of *something* off the side of a very plain, windowless structure that stood several stories taller than any of the other buildings around it.

This was the third team she'd seen at work on a building in the vicinity — the sight of the spider-legged machines picking their way up and down the sides of buildings while the humans maneuvered to pry off the — what? Paint? Billboard? Graffiti?

Whatever it was, it seemed to be of utmost importance to get it off in one very careful piece. The spiderworkers always started at the top, using what looked to Maureen like old-fashioned tools for wallpapering, as patient as sculptors, no one hurrying, all of them working at the same speed and rhythm. After awhile, the layer would peel away from the building and they would coax it along until it hit another sticking point. Then some of them would hold it in place to keep it from tearing (she supposed) while the others worked on separating it from the structure.

"Any other questions?" she said finally, turning to him.

"And the old people? Are they in school too? Everybody over the age of fifty-five back to campus for refresher math?"

"We don't know very much about how these people age," she said. "It's one of the things Judy's working on —"

"I've talked to Judy," West said impatiently

"Then you know even more than I do, at the moment," Maureen said, unperturbed. "What you have to remember is that we've never encountered a civilization quite like this, thriving in a completely sheltered interior environment. We have no idea how that might affect growth, health, aging, birth and death rates. We still haven't been able to figure out how old these people are as a civilization — all we know is they have no firsthand societal memory of any other kind of life. And since we don't know their typical life span to begin with, we can't really speculate."

She knew she was irritating the hell out of their dashing young pilot and the more callused part of her nature was all but enjoying it. Don West wanted to go flying off in all directions, setting off alarms, circling the wagons, drawing his sword, and generally putting them all on red alert and keeping them there. But that wasn't going to do a bit of good. If they weren't really in any danger, it was pointless at best. At worst, they might offend again, so badly that they ended up in danger by their own ignorance.

And if they were in some kind of jeopardy, the last thing they wanted to do was demonstrate their awareness. If they had become unwitting prisoners, the best thing would be to let their captors go on thinking they were still unwitting, so they could try to put together some kind of plan. She thought about explaining all this to Don West and decided against it for the time being.

The spider-legged mobiles changed their positions again. Two of them were rolling the substance down like a giant sheet of parchment while the other four worked at prying it off. It was a striking picture, like nothing she'd ever seen on Earth. Like nothing *anyone* had ever seen on Earth, and Don West wasn't even looking at it.

"Then where are the poor?" he demanded. "Where's the homeless?" He made a gesture at the street — for lack of a better word — and moved around in front of her to look her in the eye. "Where's the crime? What's going on?"

"I keep asking myself that," Maureen said, speaking in a low voice in the hope that that would calm him. "I won't know any answers until I can figure out how to ask the questions. However, you might think about this while we're waiting: What sort of statement is it about us and the world we come from, when we question the absence of poverty, degradation, and violence in another civilization as something suspect?"

West barely hesitated. "I don't know what it says about us or our world or even this one. But I do know a couple of things for sure and here's one: There's no such thing as Utopia for all. What one person calls Utopia, another calls hell."

Maureen had the sensation of going over a mental speed bump. "That's true," she said slowly. "And, as the daughter-in-law he never lived to meet, I recognize the source. He also said that there was no substitute for the facts — you could play hunches and follow your intuition, but when it came time to answer for your actions, you'd better be able to cough up the facts. Isn't that so?"

"John Robinson chose me for this mission in the first place because I'm *not* a slave to facts or orders. I've kept you all alive so far —"

"Well, it's not like you had to do it all alone, Major," she snapped at him.

"No, I didn't," he said sulkily. "It just felt that way." He did a perfect parade-ground about-face and strode away before she could say anything else.

Hurry, hurry, hurry, he thought, marching back toward the place where he'd left Penny. *Step right up and ride the Robinson Family Emotional Roller Coaster! Thrill to the sensation of being jerked one way and then all the way in the opposite direction, straight up, straight down, without stopping! You'll laugh, you'll scream, you'll tear your hair. You'll feel like shit, you'll get an ulcer, maybe you'll even have a stroke and die!*

It should only be that quick, he thought angrily. Not with his luck, not the way things had been going. The Robinsons were going to make sure he went as slowly and painfully as possible, each of them taking turns driving him to the thin edge of complete blow-out and then pulling him back just far enough for Smith to get in his licks before the next one started it all over again.

Jesus. *Jesus.* What was *with* that woman? You'd think she'd spent her entire life under glass like a pampered pheasant, breathing in filtered dome air and breathing out ennui.

Jesus. She hadn't managed to piss him off this much while they'd all been locked in the *Jupiter Two* together —

He bumped into someone and staggered back, nearly falling.

"Apologies." The two strong hands gripping his forearms belonged to a striking, compact woman with skin the color of antique ivory. He was about to answer with something equally innocuous when four circles faded into existence on her forehead, becoming spirals and then concentric circles as he watched.

His jaw dropped. A moment later, he collected himself and forced his gaze down a few inches to the rest of her face, where nothing half so interesting was going on, but which was attractive nonetheless.

"Sorry," he said. "I've never seen anything like that before. I didn't mean to gape."

Her head tilted slightly as she studied him. "Ah, but you could have," she said after a bit.

"Could have what?" he said, mystified. "Gaped?"

"Seen them. And had your own." She lifted one hand so that it was briefly palm-out at the base of her throat, then walked on past him. He stared after her for a moment and then made the same gesture, even though she had not turned around to see it. Maureen Robinson could have all her facts and research. There were some things you just *knew* from experience and he by God *knew* a military salute when he saw one, no matter what form it took.

Chapter Thirteen

". . . one ream of standard typing paper; one pocketscanner; one palmtop with extra batteries . . ."

John Robinson held the strip of cloth between two fingers at eye level, listening to Judy's voice, the sound small but distinct as it listed the contents of her desk back on the *Jupiter Two.*

"What *is* this?" he asked his older daughter, turning the strip one way and then the other. Judy's voice faded and came back as he did so. The cloth was flat white, six inches long, and an inch wide, and didn't seem to be any different from any other shred of cloth he'd ever come across. Except that a near-perfect reproduction of Judy's voice was issuing from it.

"It's a list of what I need from my quarters on the *Jupiter Two.*" She reached over and pinched the bottom of the strip. There was a jump in the sound, like an old-fashioned CD-ROM bouncing a laser off a scratch, and the tiny voice began the list over again from the beginning.

"No, what's *this?*" He shook the cloth slightly. "What do you call this?"

"Tape recorder?" She smiled at him. "Memo pad? Dictaphone? What they have instead of written language?"

He handed the strip to her and sat back on the

couch. The couch was one of the many similar everyday objects Maureen had prescribed as a way to prevent the onset of a homesickness-triggered depressive episode. It was covered in a deep red-brown velourish material that had him unconsciously stroking it like a cat from time to time. He did so now. "I know you'll explain," he said, feeling a nervous amusement, "so I really don't have to ask you to, do I?"

Her smile widened. "It's one of those cultural purloined letters — right out in front of you but you can't see it because your view of it is obscured by certain assumptions. It's the secret of their clothes, and why they don't bother with written language. All their cloth can record sound and play it back. Not indiscriminately — they can choose what to record. As you might imagine, a lot of them go for local news, announcements, latest music, poetry, letters, articles." She shrugged. "As you might imagine, there isn't much in the way of war and atrocity updates, traffic reports, or scandals involving movie stars and politicians."

"How did you discover this gem of a tidbit?" he asked her. "Did you overhear someone's singing shirt?"

"You almost never hear anyone's shirt singing. That's where the earphones, or ear implants come in. All the sound is conducted via contact with the body. Nobody hears it but the wearer. Except for special things like this. Most people use it to send messages to each other. You might even call it the greeting card from outer space."

He shuddered. "What a thought."

"Anyway, I mentioned to Pir, one of the people I share lab space with, that I had to make a list of things I needed or I'd keep forgetting. She gave me this and told me to talk to it. Pinch one end to start, pinch again to finish. Pinch the other end to play back."

He handed it back to her, a troubled expression clouding his face.

"What is it?" she asked him.

"Well, let's see. Where to begin?" He took a breath. "The walls may well have ears, but so does everyone's fashion statement. It explains something I saw earlier today — or a little while ago, whatever — two people talking without talking. I'd be real careful what I said to anyone about anything, anywhere, all the time. And that's before even considering the question of how we're going to find our way back to the *Jupiter Two* when our hosts deny the existence of such things without bothering to try to explain where we came from or how we got here." He took another, heavier breath. "And then there's the most dismaying thing of all."

"What?" Judy asked him, starting to look genuinely alarmed.

"*Star Songs of the Dream Dancer.* Issuing continuously and without end from Penny's entire wardrobe."

Judy rolled her eyes. "If only it were. I'm going to ask our green friend — Inrica — how to get back to the one who met us. You know, with the weird eyes. If we find him, we find the *Jupiter Two.*"

"We don't have to. Will's working on a local mapping and orientation program. He's given over part of the robot's brain to compiling it. When it's done, which it will be soon, we'll be able to find the *Jupiter Two* and possibly a whole lot more, without having to ask directions.

Judy gave a small laugh. "This isn't one of those 'men don't ask directions' things, is it?"

John laughed with her. "Maybe it is, in a way. In this case, I don't think it would be a good idea to tip our new friends off about every move we want to make."

"Good thinking." She looked at the strip of recording cloth again. "You know, I wonder if anyone ever tells lies here."

"And *I* wonder what they have instead of trust."

Father and daughter looked at each other for a long moment.

"Fashion?" she guessed.

This was *it,* Penny thought, staring up at the ever-changing hologram. Jalleril had told her the form morphed according to inputs coming from different measuring devices all over the city — temperature, humidity, percentage of carbon dioxide, noise levels — all sorts of things that would generate temporary patterns, which in turn became shapes. It was what her brother would have called a three-dimensional representation of an attractor, and what she called highly cool.

At the moment, the hologram looked a bit like a feathery tree that had gone into an insanely prolific branching sequence in the process of partially absorbing its own trunk and turning into a butterfly. It wasn't the only motion-sculpture in the gallery, but it was the most interesting, and her personal favorite.

"I love motion-sculpture," she sighed. "I love the whole idea of mutating art. I could stand here and watch this change for ages."

Beside her, Jalleril smiled. He was about her own height, with wiry black hair cut very close to his head, Oriental eyes, and deep ruby skin with a black undertone. His teeth were perfect blood-red crystals, which Penny also found highly attractive, although impossible to describe as such. She tried to imagine telling her friends back home about his red crystal smile; they'd never get it.

Penny wasn't sure whether she was in love with his smile, his velvety voice, or that remarkable ruby skin. OK, infatuated might be technically the correct term, but, really, who cared? He was great. Even better, *he* thought *she* was great and, for once, all was right with the world. Well, *this* world. *Yes, folks, there* is *life in outer space, and it's really, really good-looking.*

"I'm glad to hear you say that, because I'm the artist."

Penny's own smile deepened. "And they're already giving you gallery space to exhibit," she said, feeling both pleased and envious.

Cupping her elbow to steer her gently through the rest of the gallery, Jalleril looked puzzled. "Already?"

"Is that the wrong way to say it?" Penny asked, hoping she hadn't managed to offend him.

"It just makes it sound as if I were somehow not ready." He smoothed the white tunic he was wearing. "Surely *you're* ready?"

She started to tell him that her determination of her own readiness seldom if ever counted for much and then paused, suddenly realizing two things: first, that he had assumed she was his age — or whatever the equivalent of age was around here — although he was actually much older, and second, he didn't know the difference.

The other artists she'd met, each the color of a gemstone, some of them painters, others builders of holographic images, and some she would have called musicians rather than artists, how old had they been? Or rather, how old had they seemed?

She realized the only thought she'd given to it was to be thankful she hadn't been dumped into a group of little kids, which was what usually happened when she went somewhere for the first time. People were always taking her to be younger than she really was, just because she wasn't as tall as Judy or as filled-out as some other girls her age.

Here, however, she'd been brought to a group of adults — real adults, not just older kids whose intelligence and abilities overshot their age group. So what that there weren't any kids here on her level?

Or did it mean there weren't any kids here at all?

The chill this idea gave her was followed by another as she sneaked a look at Jalleril, who had used her elbow to move her a little closer to him. *He doesn't know I'm just a kid. He couldn't tell the difference between me and Judy and Mom!*

She attempted to move away from him without seeming to, but he assumed she was simply trying to steer them toward another exhibit, this one a transparent globe with something that looked vaguely organic spreading over the inside from the bottom up. She'd seen that stuff somewhere before but she was too agitated at the moment to try remembering where and filed it away for later contemplation.

Contemplation — something else they were supposed to do, according to that weird alien. She brushed the thought away — there didn't seem to be much opportunity for them to try folding themselves into the lotus position right now.

". . . to live now?" Jalleril was saying.

"I'm sorry — I — I got so involved looking at that —" she lied, pointing at the globe.

Jalleril's red crystal smile was even broader. Did anything *ever* upset this guy? "We'll all eat that later, when it's ready. I'm glad you'll be here for it. I said, do you want to see where you're going to live now?"

A hard lump of uneasiness was forming slowly in her chest. "I already have a place to live. I'm with my family."

He looked surprised. "Are you being punished?"

She laughed out loud and then stopped quickly when she saw he wasn't trying to be funny. "No. No, I'm not being punished. We just — We just live together. It's the way we do things." He was still bewildered. "Why would you think I was being punished?"

"Why else would you be confined to your immediate pool of origin?"

She gave another short laugh. "I'm not being confined. Nobody is. We just — We're family. We live together, we always have. We came here that way."

Now he looked troubled. "Are you somehow . . ." he searched for a word, "Incomplete? Unfinished?"

A warning bell went off in her mind. She pretended to study the globe full of moss to cover her increasing uneasiness. "I don't know. I don't *think* so, but could you tell if I was?"

"Usually you can. Not that it happens very often, it's just not — well, *decent.* Watching someone *change.* Come to maturity. Every so often, somebody who thinks no one's ever been shocked before gets permission to decant a viable organism still in the depths of immaturity, and then walks it around calling it an interactive display. Supposedly it's to make people face the facts of their origins but I think it's just . . . filth posing as art."

"Really." Penny folded her arms and hoped he couldn't see that she was shaking a little.

"What happens to the person afterwards? When the so-called artist is through with the display, or when maturity sets in? What would you do, what *could* you do with yourself? Further development is impossible. You can try to learn something but there's no way you can ever reach the level of the properly matured. You'll always be stunted. But not the artist — the artist never has to suffer, just the 'artwork'. That kind of a thing is *that* to visit on a person and call it *art?*"

"Total trash," Penny said. "Actually, what I'm doing is, I'm compiling a musical kind of spectrum of . . . of the biological elements that we all share, but that have come out differently, you know. . . and then I'm going to, um, chart the, the number of steps each one of us takes per day and, um, well, you'll see. It's going to be very intricate."

"I can tell," Jalleril said approvingly. "After you're finished, you'll probably be relieved to choose new living space." He took hold of her elbow again and steered her out of the gallery and onto the balcony walkway.

The walkway was a wide ribbon of the plastic-like material that served as paving here. It spiraled around the transparent needle-shaped gallery building, which housed a wildly eclectic collection of galleries and studios. As you progressed from the top of the building, where they had been, to the bottom, you had your choice of enjoying the cityscape in a full 360-degree view or peering into each gallery or studio and watching whatever there was to see — a new installation, someone going at a work in progress, other things Penny wasn't sure how to categorize. Privacy was something else they came at in such a completely different way that she couldn't be sure she had even begun to understand what they meant by it.

But never mind that — What would happen if they found out she and Will were 'unfinished'? From the way Jalleril had talked about it, that had to be a much more serious offense than Smith's faux pas with the glowing woman.

And then, as she gazed out over the cityscape, another thought occurred to her. If people weren't *decent* until they were fully developed, where *were* they while they did develop?

She remembered the word Jalleril had used: *decant.* What had he said exactly? Something about "decanting a viable organism."

Decant as in *pour from a bottle?*

"I'm inspired," she said suddenly, pulling away from Jalleril. "I'm going to go home and do some charting."

He looked disappointed and she was annoyed

with herself for feeling a pull of attraction. “Until, then.”

“Yes,” she said, backing away and smiling. “Until.” She had to force herself not to pelt down the walkway hollering for her mother.

Chapter Fourteen

The sight of Judy asleep on the couch made Maureen pause in the doorway, caught between surprise at finding her there and worry that something bad might have happened to John or the children. Mother reflexes — once you had them, you had them, and you couldn't outgrow them, outrun them, or forget then. There was no such thing as an ex-mother.

It seemed to her at the moment that Judy's sleeping face hadn't changed since her baby days. Maureen could remember cradling her in one arm while she balanced a notebook on her opposite knee, paging through the results of the latest environment studies. Back in the days when they'd still believed there was time to turn things around for planet Earth. It hadn't been long after that, though, that they'd understood they were beaten.

Still, the sight of her firstborn asleep brought back the memory of a time in her life when hope had been more abundant. Of course, it was probably like that for most parents — first child, early days, good days. The nostalgia tightened her throat.

Then her surroundings came back into focus around her. *Shake it off, Mommy. Later, if you live through this, you can shut yourself away with every-*

body's baby books and have yourself a good cry.

Shutting the door behind her, she leaned over Judy, about to touch her when she saw the strip of cloth lying across her daughter's palm. Curious, she picked it up and held it at eye level.

"Half a dozen waterproof pens," Judy's voice recited, "one ream of standard typing paper, one pocket —"

"Oh hi," Judy said, sitting up and yawning. "I put Dad to bed. He was forgetting to sleep. So was I. It's hard to remember when you don't have the visual cues of day and night. I guess I never realized how much of our sleeping and waking habits is down to conditioning." She yawned again. "Don't know why. That summer I spent in Oslo, I remember staying up for days."

Maureen sat down next to her and dangled the cloth strip questioningly.

"As I was explaining to Dad, a fashion statement in this town is a literal thing."

Maureen listened as Judy told her about the unique characteristics of the local clothing. That explained the near silence the people in the spider-walkers had managed to maintain throughout their task. They'd probably been transmitting to each other via their clothing. Had to be. Kept the noise level down, certainly, and in an enclosed environment, that would be a real concern.

She was about to get up and check on John when Judy went on to tell her about her conversation with Don West.

"I saw our flyboy," Maureen told her. "I don't think my answers were enough for him. And now I don't think they're enough for me, either."

"I've done a lot of thinking about it since I talked to Don," Judy said. "Later on, I went back to the lab and tried a little leading conversation on Wann and Pir but I didn't learn much. I don't think." She sighed. "There's so much *stuff* embedded in what people say to each other, in *any* culture, not just this one. And in this one, we're getting it all at a remove anyway, because it has to be translated."

"Which is something else that's been nagging at me," Maureen said. "We need translators to understand them and vice versa."

Judy looked over at her and nodded. "Right. But they've all got translators already, which begs the question: How many different languages can they possibly have among them if they all live in one city."

"I don't know," John said from the doorway to the bedroom, "but so far, I'd swear there's only one. One *spoken* language." He shuffled around to the couch and sat down on Maureen's left. "I did a crazy thing today. I mean, a little while ago, it's all today here, isn't it? Anyway, I went out without my translator."

"Risky," Maureen acknowledged. "But I wish I'd thought of that myself."

"Any time they talk, it sounds like the same language to me, though I can't say that maybe it isn't just similar, like Norwegian and Swedish, or Mandarin and Cantonese."

"But if they are languages that are that close, then they *should* understand each other well enough, they shouldn't need translators. Waste of effort," Judy said. "And if it's the *same* language, then what in God's name do they need translators *for?*"

"Surveillance," Maureen and John said together. Maureen turned to look at her husband with wry amusement. "Got dam ol' cozmic paranoia blues again."

"We wouldn't be paranoid if they weren't after us," he said. His smile faded. "That would explain the grunt and gesture I saw. But the next question is: If they know that, why do they hold skill for it?"

"Why did we hold still for practices that we knew would make our air unbreathable?" Maureen said. "Answer: Because more people in power were benefitting from it than not. This must be profitable somehow for some very powerful people, who have convinced your basic citizen that what's good for the big guys is good for the little guys." She allowed herself a small laugh. "Besides, what if it *does* translate once in a while? Maybe it's a sure way of avoiding misunderstandings. Keeps the peace that way. Maybe in a closed-in place like this, they think surveillance is a small price to pay to avoid conflicts that could turn violent. When we left Earth, there were enough people in Houston alone who honestly believed that if you were innocent and had nothing to hide, you wouldn't object to having your privacy violated regularly and even without warning."

"Well, I never thought much of that frame of mind," Judy said. "I don't think I'd be too thrilled to spend the rest of my life in a whole society that thought that way. I know, I know —" She held up both hands. "Where are we going to go, and how?"

"I don't know," John said, "but I think we should start looking for those answers." His troubled expression deepened. "And speaking of more things to worry about, where's Smith?"

"If I'd realized this was a bloody welfare state," Smith muttered to himself, "I'd have done *everything* differently."

The view from the penthouse was marvelous, but then, the view from a penthouse was supposed to be marvelous. That was the whole point. He could imagine the Robinsons oohing and ahhing over it as if they'd never seen anything from a great height before. But it took a lot more than a mere panorama to make Zachary Smith's day. A hefty supply of the Kiss was a good place to start; a hefty supply of customers willing to part with hefty supplies of the local currency-equivalent was a good place to get to. Repeat as desired; that will be all, thank you.

Well, at least he had the hefty supply of the Kiss. The fact that money seemed to be not only unnecessary but practically unknown was going to screw up the rest of it.

He sank deeper in the plush velvety chair. It was vaguely chair-shaped, anyway, and highly comfortable, perfect for enjoying the Kiss. A shame he just couldn't enjoy it at all now. Or not as much as he should have been able to, anyway.

He peered through the shifting patterns and pulsating colors that dominated his vision at the rest of the people in the room. There seemed to be more of them, but he wasn't sure. That was the thing about being Kissed here — their own colors could make them hard to distinguish among the drug's special effects. He was having trouble now — there might have been thirty people or a hundred. The original three he'd been dealing with were somewhere among them, he supposed. The gathering had been their idea — bring together all the people who would be distributing the Kiss, introduce them to the product, send them off with a supply.

And then what? Nothing. They just came back for more when they ran out, world without end. Why not just give it to everyone with their soap ration? There was no point to this, Smith thought disgustedly. Where there was no money, there was no greed, and drugdealing depended on greed — greed, gratification, and paranoia, to be precise.

So here he was, stuck with manufacturing and distributing a product for nothing. The only good thing about it was that he'd have an almost unlimited supply for himself, but with the stock on the *Jupiter Two*, he'd had that to begin with, and he hadn't had to share it with anyone then.

He turned his head away from the other people in the room and stared out at the city. Strange music was running through his mind; occasionally, that happened when he was Kissed. Some media player in his brain would click on and run through a repertoire he hadn't realized he still remembered. He let it play on in the background, something produced in some kind of melodious percussion, and stared at the outline of buildings against what they saw instead of sky.

Again, the light and color varied, but it never seemed to get any darker out there than late afternoon. Shadows were always soft because the light came from many sources, all of them diffuse. It did change over periods of time but so far he hadn't been able to determine the interval. No, scratch that — he hadn't bothered trying. All he knew for sure was that they didn't spend a lot of time sleeping around here.

They weren't much for eating, either, as near as he could tell. The most interesting meal he'd had here had been with the glowing woman, and that had ended badly. In the city, they only seemed to nibble at cracker or dumpling kinds of things. Hardly worth the bother of eating. No wonder they needed the Kiss. He was surprised there weren't more drugs.

But there had to be, he realized. Any society advanced enough to have medicine had drugs.

Where were the doctors, the pharmacists? Where were the hospitals, what did they do with their sick? What did they do with their *dead?*

He started to sit up straight and then fell back again. Oh, for God's sake, what did *he* care? He wasn't planning to be sick *or* dead. St. Judy already had laboratory space, let *her* cure their common colds and their cancers. He had resigned from the active practice of medicine the night he had inadvertently stowed away on the *Jupiter Two.*

Then he was sitting up again, but this time because someone was pulling him forward. The pale-green man, one of the people he had dealt with originally — what did he call himself? Menal? Manal? Manilla?

Another face shimmered beside his, this one the color of old parchment. It even had writing on it. No, designs, symbols of some kind. Tattoos? Except they were moving. Or maybe not, perhaps that was just the Kiss.

"I think your friend is quite intoxicated," said the decorated face.

"He calls it being Kissed," the pale-green man answered.

The decorated face was amused. "And that was what he offered? A Kiss?"

"Well, *we* like it." The green man laughed. "However, after he finished telling us his story, I knew you would want me to contact you."

"Good mind." A hand came out of the roiling colors that made up Smith's vision and tapped his right cheek a few times. "Which is more than I can say for our friend."

"He's acceptably intelligent when he's not Kissed," the green man said. "Although he seems to have no morals. You will probably want to put him to sleep afterwards."

"Yes, a hiatus with correction and restabilizing will do him a world of good. And it will do us a whole *universe* of good."

The green man must have seen something in his expression, Smith thought, though he could not have said at that moment whether he was smiling, frowning, or even crying. The Kiss was extraordinarily strong in him. "Perhaps we shouldn't talk where he can hear us."

"Forget it. *He* will." Decorated Face let him slump back against the chair. "Right now, he couldn't tell you who *he* is, let alone who *we* are. He'll never know. He'll take us right to this 'jupiter' and hand it over, all of it. It'll work beautifully. We gain a universe and we gain the power. After the first hyperjump, *no one* will want to risk displeasing us. We can give this Kiss to those who behave. Exile for those who don't — dump them on one of those worlds of surface-dwellers and watch them clinging to the ground in terror that they'll fall into the sky."

The two of them stood up and their voices faded slightly. Smith managed to roll his head around so that he was looking up at them.

"I always *knew* there was something more," said the pale-green man.

"That's an easy one," the decorated face said dismissively. "It's learning how best to make use of it that takes real intelligence."

They moved away from him, leaving him draped over the chair, trying to get his numb lips to form the word *Judy*.

Chapter Fifteen

The other people in the lab had paid no attention to him in all the time he'd been there, and Will wasn't sure whether to be relieved or alarmed. He could imagine what his father would have said about that: *Might as well be relieved, because you don't need any more bad news.*

According to the robot's self-contained clock, he had worked steadily for three hours, with only a few bathroom breaks. The robot's twin had provided a local map in its memory, giving him the location of the bathrooms. Those, at least, were reassuringly familiar; apparently humanoid mammals tended toward the same answers to questions of hygiene.

Now he was starting to feel hungry, and he couldn't find any reference in the memory to any place like a restaurant, or even the local version of a vending machine. Restaurants were nonexistent — these people didn't eat for the sake of socializing, or vice versa. But then, he'd tasted the food so that wasn't exactly a mystery to him.

What was a mystery to him, however, was how they'd come to such a sorry pass, as Dr. Smith would have put it. Dr. Smith was a world-class jerk — make that universe-class — but some of the things he came up with no one had ever said better.

His mother had said something about looking into their system of food production. What she really needed was a map like the one he'd found in the twin robot's navigational archives. It showed not only all the buildings and the lanes, or whatever you called indoor streets, but how each building was laid out, and where the power centers were located in each one. Except this map was limited to the area between where they were living and this building, where he was supposed to work on his AI project.

Still, fiddling with the settings, he'd managed to project a 3-D tankless image of the building's schematics, superimposing the plumbing over the architectural drawing. It wasn't the sort of thing that would have fascinated him normally, except that the schematic included far more area below the city's designated ground level than even an especially deep basement would have accounted for. But all the detail had been stripped out of it, leaving a featureless blank. It wasn't a power plant or a water supply — he'd already found those. Projected future expansion? Storm shelter?

Oh yeah, right. Like they had tornadoes here everyday. It was more likely to have something to do with strange religious customs. Every building with its own chapel so no one ever had to miss services just because they were at work. Chapel, altar, incense, prayerbooks, and, further down, a graveyard. He'd seen stranger things with his own eyes. Well, maybe equally strange, anyway.

The original robot came to life behind him. *"Robot has detected a source of more detailed information accessible via that unit."*

Will turned around to look at it. "How do I get it?"

"Robot must do it for you."

A hard line of blue light passed from the twin's dome into the original robot's. Will heard the processors hit maximum and sink back within the space of a second, before the blue light flashed in reverse.

"Try it now," the robot told him.

"What did you do?" Will asked.

"The map data was compressed. Robot retranslated it so that it is no longer compressed."

The twin obediently projected the new map for him. Will's mouth dropped open.

"Turn it off," he said to the twin.

The hologram vanished, Will turned to the original robot again. "You said you retranslated the data. Are you sure you did it right?"

"Robot uncompressed what there was. There is no extraneous information."

"Can you read that?"

"Robot has already read it."

Will took a breath. "Then can you tell me if those are what I think they are under the building?"

"Only if you tell Robot what you think they are."

He lowered his voice and moved closer to the robot. "Are those figures really *bodies?*"

"Affirmative."

Will took a breath. *Jeez.* "Is there any information as to why these people bury their dead rather than cremate them?"

"Error, Will Robinson. Bodies under the building are not dead."

Will had the sensation that the room had tilted sideways. "What — What are they?" he asked after a long, dizzy moment.

"Waiting," the robot said.

He stole a look around the room. Some of the people had left without him noticing. No one was paying attention to him.

"What are they waiting for?" he asked.

This time, it was the twin robot that answered.

"Their turn," it said.

She'd have sworn that he was too wrecked to go anywhere, Judy thought, looking around the empty apartment. She was sure she had the right place — she remembered the couch. Apparently she'd gotten too high-handed with him and he'd upped stakes for wherever it was the drug addicts hung out.

Great bedside manner, Doc. You really turned his life around. She pushed the thought away. Later, she could beat herself up over this. Right now, she had to find him, sober him up, and see if he knew anything useful. The chances were actually good that he did, if he had made contact with anything like a criminal or underground element. Those were the people who usually knew the most about how any social system was put together, since they spent so much time climbing around on the edges. The thing was, Smith was so drug-addled, he might not realize he knew anything at all.

And now that she thought of how drug-addled he was, why was she assuming that he'd moved out voluntarily?

She could picture it several different ways: Smith decides to share his treasure with someone congenial. Or — more likely — Smith decides to *sell* some of his treasure. Only how do you sell something in a moneyless society?

How about this one: Smith trades some drug for access to something he wants . . . a way to make more. Or a way to get back to Earth?

All right, that last didn't seem terribly likely, given that the people here didn't believe in the universe as it was, and Smith didn't know enough about the *Jupiter Two* to fly it himself even if they had.

No. Most likely, Smith had decided to play Drug Kingpin — here, try this, have as much as you want, just give me everything I need to make more — and someone had decided to show him a new spot in the hierarchy: unpaid slave, maybe.

While you're at it, here's another interesting thing to think about: If he did leave involuntarily, do you think whoever helped him on his way might be watching the place to see if anyone else is interested in him?

Behind her, she could hear the front door opening.

So, had Judy found the place empty and gone looking for Smith, or had they left together? Don West moved past the couch and into the next room. A pad on the floor had no dent in the middle to indicate that Smith had slept there recently; the bathroom was also empty. He went back into the front room, scanning the bare floor as if some clue might start fading into existence if he kept looking at it.

Depressing place, all told. Of all of them, Smith seemed to have made the least amount of effort to be at home. On the other hand, none of them had gone back to the *Jupiter Two* to fetch any of their belongings yet, so they'd all been living a rather spartan style. But Smith had made no effort at all; the place had less character than a prison cell.

A prison cell. Maybe Smith had managed to screw up good this time and get himself arrested. Whatever that entailed. Whatever it was, Smith could probably manage it with his eyes closed and one hand tied behind his back. But had he also managed to get Judy into trouble as well? That was the million-dollar question. The million-dollar answer, of course, was: All too likely. If only he'd gotten back to the Robinsons before Judy had gone off looking for Smith.

He plumped down on the couch and drummed his fingers on the wide stuffed arm. Something shifted under his fingertips and he paused, capturing it between his index and middle fingers.

A strip of cloth. Nothing really, but it looked like it was supposed to be something. Something torn off a shirt in a struggle maybe? He held it up to examine it.

". . . fly it. No one knows how except Don West," Judy's voice said, sounding small and a bit filtered, but otherwise completely identifiable. It took him a moment to realize it was coming from the cloth strip. "If you want to go anywhere, you'll have to convince him. He's not going to be a terribly easy sell."

Another voice answered, but it was too faint for Don to make out the words. Judy's voice came back.

"I'm not going —"

There was a moment of nothing, followed by Judy's voice again, this time speaking slowly and clearly: ". . . one palmtop with extra batteries, one pair of infrared goggles . . ." Then it stopped altogether.

He stared at the strip, turning it carefully one way and then another, looking for anything that even suggested circuits. Whatever the bug was, it was too small to see with the naked eye. Maybe one of the Robinsons could figure this one.

Chapter Sixteen

The first slap didn't feel real, but the second one did.

Even so, it took a few seconds for Judy's face to come into focus for him, and when it did he wasn't happy. He felt as if someone had been jack-hammering on the top of his head for most of a day.

"Smith, you worthless piece of *crap.*"

Yes, she was definitely there, he wasn't hallucinating or dreaming. "What?" he said hoarsely. "Lemme 'lone. Not s'posed a be here." He pushed at her weakly with one hand. God, but he was sick. He needed a dose bad. Where was his vial?

"You've gotten us all into a really good one now —"

She yammered on and on and he tried like mad to shut her out while he patted himself down. He couldn't find his vial, for God's sake. He wasn't going to care about anything if he couldn't find his vial. If it wasn't in one of his pockets, then he had to get up and look for it and he wasn't in any shape right now to do that. He needed to rest. If he could take a nap, he would feel better. Then he could cope.

He rolled over to get away from her, wrapping his arms around his head. After awhile, her voice faded and he felt himself drift away.

"We are quite cramped in this little world," the pale-green man said, "and have been for a long time. The belief of the general population is that this is the sole environment that can support life, and there is nowhere else to go. You can help us prove otherwise. It is vital to our survival as a species, a civilization, that we do so."

Judy nodded. Through the doorway behind the man, she could see Smith sprawled on the floor-pad. He hadn't so much as twitched for a long time now, though if she watched carefully, she could see that he was still breathing. She could almost have hoped his addiction had finished him off.

Moving in what she hoped was a casual way, she planted her left elbow in her right hand and leaned her chin on her left fist, speaking as close to the scrap of cloth hidden there as she could. If her theory about one fragment transmitting to another was correct, she could at least warn everyone. Provided her mother or father found the shred she had left behind before any of the locals did.

"And I keep telling you, all you had to do was talk to my father. You don't have to hold me and Dr. Smith here like prisoners. Just let me contact him. He'll come here, lay out the whole hyperdrive for you, and you can go anywhere you want."

"We have no raw materials to create a little world like yours — a 'spaceship' — or a hyperdrive."

"My father can help you with that, too. We all can —"

"No." That strange parchment-colored woman with the facial tattoos looked up from the touch-screen in her lap. "We can't risk our resources. In particular, we can't take chances with the structure. Whether we had it bestowed on us by a supreme being or whether it was built by our ancestors — who may or may not have been surface-dwellers on some other world — one miscalculation in density or pressure and the whole thing implodes. Would *you* take a chance of destroying *your* world?"

Judy shook her head, bewildered. "But then what are you going to use for fuel?"

"Fuel we still have plenty of," the green man said. "There *are* those who believe the power lines are artificial and not the gift of an all-wise, all-merciful, and loving god" — he glanced at the tattooed woman, who looked amused — "but in the end it doesn't matter. Our power lines have maintained us."

Power lines? Judy frowned. She couldn't remember seeing anything so much as an extension cord, let alone high-tension wires —

The image of the world as they had approached it popped into her memory, the glowing lines etched on the metal, converging in a spot that Penny had thought looked like a target. A network of energy collectors, perhaps initially charged by some cataclysm, like a nova, and then just kept up as the world journeyed through the universe. Except here it was in interstellar space, with the nearest stars — that is, power source — light-years away. And this world didn't travel at the speed of light, not nearly.

"You're starting to run low," she blurted. "The lines aren't recharging the way they're supposed to, because this part of the universe really is the void. There's nothing here."

The tattooed woman set her touch-screen aside, got up, and went over to Judy, leaning one hand on the arm of her chair and looking at her closely. "For someone whose specialty is mere body maintenance, you're actually quite intelligent, aren't you?"

Before Judy could think how to respond, the woman grabbed her left hand, pried her fingers open and snatched the fragment of cloth away from her. Judy could only stare in amazement.

"Your people must be very furtive and devious," the tattooed woman said to her disapprovingly. "You're always trying to hide things from everyone else. A highly civilized society feels no need to conceal anything. We live on a level of freedom that you'll never know."

"This is a very small world compared to mine," Judy said. "You have plenty of room for everyone as far as I can see. My world was — is — crowded. In a crowded world, people come to value privacy. The right to be left alone. Not watched all the time, not listened-in on."

The tattooed woman looked back at the green

man. "This world is more crowded than you know. We just happen to be between cycles at the moment. Like you, we discovered that, while it may not be the most desirable solution for the problem of how to conserve resources and reduce wear and tear on one's environment, it is the least odious. And it does actually prolong their lives."

"What does?" Judy asked, baffled.

"Hibernation. What do *you* call it — cold sleep? Deep sleep? Suspension within life-support?" The tattooed woman leaned closer "We're anxious to see if your method uses more power than ours and, if so, is it better or just greedy?"

"So who are you going to put into hibernation, and when?" Judy said. "I don't —"

The tattooed woman laughed. "We're not *going* to put anyone in hibernation. They're all already *in* hibernation. But it's almost time for the start of the next cycle. We'll be getting them out soon."

"But . . ." Judy looked from the woman to the green man and back again. "I've never seen *any* hibernation capsules."

"No. You haven't."

"Now who's being devious and furtive?" Judy said evenly.

"We're an open society," the woman said. "You're just not a member."

"Yet," added the green man.

"There's a piece missing off the end,"

Maureen Robinson said, holding the strip of cloth in her palm. "I'm not sure how much."

"You think she tore it off deliberately, or it happened when she struggled?" Don asked.

Maureen shook her head. "Will could probably figure out how to amplify the voice we can't hear. That might tell us something."

"If that's Smith," Don said, almost conversationally, "I'll personally rip his arms and legs off. Slowly. And with a sense of accomplishment."

"Get back in line," John Robinson said, his expression pained. He looked around the room they had been tempted to accept as home. What could they have been thinking of? No, all right — what had *he* been thinking?

He felt a touch on his shoulder and turned to find Maureen next to him. She slipped an arm around his waist. "When we got here, we were shell-shocked, crazy with cabin fever, and on the verge of giving up. Judy told me she had actually prepared syringes for all of us. So that when the end came, we would all sleep through it."

"Uh . . . *all* of us?" Don West asked, sounding a bit queasy.

Maureen's smile was wry. "Even Smith."

John had the sudden strong urge to catch her up in his arms and promise that he would never again let anything of the sort overtake them, that they would all protect each other, not just from outside threats, but from themselves as well. But that was the sort of promise you had to make after you were sure you were going to survive, and they were still quite a way from that point. He looked at Don West, who was still grimacing with disgust.

"You said you could find Penny and Will?"

"If they're still there," Don said.

"Then find them and bring them back here. I'm —"

"No," said Maureen. "Not here. Take them to the *Jupiter Two.*" She looked from Don West to John. "Will can find it."

"You seem awful sure of that," said Don West, sounding a good deal less sure.

"She is. So am I," said John.

"OK," Don said. "And how will *you* find it?"

"You'll send the robot back here to us," John said. "With the map, or whatever Will puts in to locate it for us."

Don hesitated. "Why don't you just come with me?"

"They might already be on their way back here," Maureen said. "If they are, and you miss them, we'll be here."

He was about to say something else; John cut him off. "It's a finite world, Major. Somehow or other, we'll find our way back to it." He jerked his chin at the door.

"I'd prefer something more concrete than 'somehow or other,' " West said, "but all right." He paused. "What about Judy?"

John felt his expression harden. "I imagine we'll be meeting her at the *Jupiter* as well."

"You imagine?" Don West paused. "Or you hope?"

"I'll get back to you on that," John said. "You just get back to the *Jupiter.*"

Chapter Seventeen

Her sense of direction seemed to have improved a great deal, Penny thought with some relief as she stopped across from the building where they had been given a place to live. It helped that the light didn't change much, which also made her wonder how these people would have reacted to a power failure. They'd probably think it was the end of everything. But then, in a completely enclosed world like this, it probably would be.

She shuddered. Somehow, this place made her feel much more claustrophobic than the *Jupiter Two* had. That didn't make any sense, since the *Jupiter* was so much smaller.

And then again, maybe she was getting claustrophobia mixed up with just having the creeps. As much as her family got on her nerves, and as much as she still hated the *Jupiter Two* mission — more than ever, come to that — at least there wasn't anything inherently wrong with just being a kid.

Was that because the limits on resources were so obvious, she wondered, or was it something even weirder and more obscure, maybe even religious? She tried to imagine what a society where everyone was born adult would really be like.

Her mother, she thought, would *freak.*

And what would *that* be like? Supercompetent, completely on her game Maureen Robinson, freaked out.

It would probably be a lot like having a blackout here, Penny thought, heading for the front door.

Don West came out then, pushing through the swinging door harder than was strictly necessary, in a rush and obviously worried. Penny started to call out to him just as he turned and saw her.

His expression changed from worried to highly alarmed, and she saw him reach into his leather jacket for his weapon.

Something caught her hard in the middle of her back and just under her jaw, around her throat. Her feet left the ground; she couldn't breathe.

Will hated the idea of giving up the robot's twin. It was deftly made; some of the hardware was lighter and better than the alloys and plastics of the original. The neural network wasn't quite as complex, but he could have fixed that. It would have been a good way of trying out certain programming experiments without risking the original's arrangement. At the very least, he could have mined it for spare parts.

Regret is a luxury that only the living may indulge in. Something Don West had said to his father right after their last hyperspace jump. The idea, Don said, was first you did whatever you could to stay alive. Then later you could luxuriate in regret for not being able to do something else.

OK, Don, he said to himself, *I just hope I'm right. If I'm not, I'm gonna look pretty goofy.*

He sent the twin on its way and had the original guide him not out of the building but further down, below it, to the grid arrangement of passageways copied from the robot's twin.

Judy had been unprepared for the rush of emotion she felt at the sight of the *Jupiter Two* as they came to the end of the tunnel. Held between two other parchment-colored, tattooed people and marched along behind the pale-green man and the first tattooed woman, she concentrated on the extra cache of weapons Don had insisted on. Weapons within reach no matter where you were on the ship — and one weapon for each of them hidden so that none of the others knew where it was. At the time, she'd found the whole idea ridiculous. Paranoia induced by toxic levels of testosterone was the way she had described it to her father, and if you factored in cabin fever, it was dangerous besides. But her father had gone along with it anyway, so that the only person who didn't know where all the weapons were was Smith.

Well, never mind. All she had to do was get them to take her aboard the *Jupiter* with them. Then she could wait for an opportunity.

Twisting around, she looked behind and was startled to see that the pale-green man and woman who'd had Smith between them were no longer there.

"Where's Zack?" she said. "Dr. Smith. The man who gave you the drug —"

"*I* remember who he is, although *he* may not." The green man laughed. "We're done with him, and he can be of no more use to you. We're putting him away."

The entryway to the *Jupiter Two* was still open, she saw, and the inside looked the same. Emotion rushed through her again, stronger this time. She recognized it as a deep and powerful desire to be among familiar surroundings again, the hunger of the exile for home and all the things of home. The sensation was strong enough to bring on vertigo; her vision seemed to distort, as if she were suddenly seeing everything through a lens shaped like a spoon, and she stumbled.

They dragged her through the entryway and onto the bridge, let her fall into Don's chair and left her there. The blast shields were lowered and she could see, through the forward windows, the alien that had first met them, standing perfectly still some distance off, watching impassively.

People hydroponics was the term that occurred to Will as he and the robot descended through the levels on the platform. Every level was apparently laid out identically — barrels of what Will assumed must be nutrients running tubes into a sort of treelike structure and, hanging from the branches, things that looked like giant egg sacs. Except these were transparent, and you could see the people curled up inside each one.

If he had simply heard about this and not seen it for himself, he'd have been grossed out to the point of being sick to his stomach. But it didn't really look all that gross. They were just people, this was suspended animation done a different way. Nothing to get grossed out over, really. He wondered what they would have made of the cryotubes Judy had developed.

"Next level stop," the robot said, and the platform slowed, coming to a smooth, gradual halt even with the floor.

"Are you sure?" Will said. "It doesn't seem like we've gone down far enough."

"This is the level," the robot said.

Will hesitated, looking around. There was no one else here besides him and the robot — no one else awake, that was. However this system worked, it didn't require caretakers.

"Surveillance?" he asked the robot.

"Each citizen is monitored internally for signs of distress or waking," the robot told him.

"How about alarms?"

"None."

"Robot guards?"

"None."

"Motion detectors?"

"None."

Will shook his head, still not quite daring to

step off the platform into the room. "I wonder why not."

"Who would break in here? There is nothing to steal except the people themselves."

Will turned to look at the robot. "Did you figure this out yourself?"

"No. The other robot supplied that information."

"How? I don't remember you guys having coffee together or anything."

"Humor by way of imagining the incongruous," said the robot matter-of-factly. *"Much information was exchanged by this unit with the other. It came with the map data. There is no perceived danger here, no need for it to be under guard. To the best of their knowledge, they are alone."* The robot rolled forward and gently nudged him off the platform. *"We must reach the* Jupiter Two, *Will Robinson. Sensors indicate life-forms are aboard now."*

"Who?" Will asked as the robot led him along an aisle between the bases of the "trees."

"Only one life-form is recognizable as Judy," the robot said, and Will was sure that he wasn't imagining that it sounded urgent. *"Others are life-forms from this world. All are in an agitated state."*

"We don't go into the military here," the woman said to Don West. Her grip on Penny's throat had loosened a little, but only a little. Penny had no doubt that this woman would squeeze the life out of her without a second thought if she judged that the situation called for it. What scared her far more, however, was knowing that the woman wouldn't feel one way or another about it if that was what she had to do. It was all the same to her. As far as Penny was concerned, that was the worst sort of grown-up. She would rather deal with Smith, who at least had weaknesses you could try to appeal to.

Mixed into the steady hum of fear in her brain was a sudden sense of pride in her own insight. *I've just* got *to remember this,* she said to herself. Star Songs of the Dream Dancer: Book the Second, the Human Spirit Cycle. *It'll be a classic.*

"It's the military that goes into us," the woman went on. "Or rather, it's already in us. Dedication — it's not just for gene pools, but it works best that way."

She was standing beside the chair Penny would have found uncomfortable in any circumstances. This room was located one level below the street, in what would have been the basement of the building where the Robinsons had so briefly lived. It showed signs of long habitation, a shabbiness of regular use, although it was basically a monk's cell — a pallet on the floor, a chair, a box the size of the trunk in her room on the *Jupiter Two.* Don West was sitting on the box, one ankle crossed over his knee, occasionally looking at his weapon lying on the floor in front of Penny. Close enough for her to kick over to him. *Maybe* close enough. She looked from him to the weapon and back again. If only they could have signaled each other in some way. Then she would know if she should try kicking it over to him, and when.

"Hash marks on the face, that's a pretty wild touch," Don said. "Does that come with the dedication? Or do you have to earn them?"

"Some of each," the woman said, sounding slightly impressed. "Some for identity, some for personal history, some to indicate qualification."

"What do you qualify for?" Don asked her.

"Saving your formation, and helping you leave here alive." The woman paused. In spite of everything, Penny twisted around to look up at her hopefully. The woman smiled down at her just as if she hadn't had her hand around the front of her throat. "Any questions?"

"About a million of them," Penny croaked, and felt the hand ease up slightly more. "How, why, who are you, all that stuff."

"You're a lively little strain, aren't you?" The woman looked from Penny to Don and back again. "Or I should say *strains,* shouldn't I. Because you and you are from the same general pool, but are otherwise unconnected. Aren't you?"

"Can you tell by looking?" asked Don.

"It is probably much more obvious to me, because there *are* so few differences here. Though we still retain enough variants that we can, and do, brew strains that are unrelated to each other, and then mix them later, if needed."

"What are you talking about?" Penny demanded.

"Genetics," Don said. "They breed on purpose here. The way they used to breed championship livestock back on Earth — horses, dogs, cats, pigs —"

"It's an all but closed system," the woman said, talking over him. "And in such circumstances, letting nature, as you call it, take its course is negligence. Our continued survival as a species depends on maintaining a population that can thrive in its circumstances."

"Or finding a way out of your circumstances," Don added. "Like getting a hyperdrive and finding worlds you can settle on."

"When that time is right," the woman said, "that's what we'll do. This is not the time."

"Why not?" Don asked. "And exactly who determines that?"

"We have a hierarchy," she said. "They are not for you to be concerned with. They interfere as little as possible, preferring to see people regulate themselves. Based on what they've observed, they mix new strains, and try them out in a separate area, to see what they might make of their lives, were they given any."

Don frowned, confused, and Penny felt a surge of triumph. "Is that why they glow?" she asked, pulling away slightly from the woman's hand. "Because they're experiments?"

The woman's facial tattoos seemed to darken as she smiled her approval at Penny. "There have been escapes into the general population in the past. The most efficient way of tracking them is simply to make them glow. It takes no energy, no extra electronics."

Penny glanced at Don, who nodded at her. "So what about those other creatures? The ones with the weird eyes?"

The woman stared at her for a moment. "Do you know that not everyone believes in them? Some of the people here think they're scare stories, made up just to keep people in line."

Penny turned to Don again, but he shook his head. "Forget it. So how are you going to help us get our ship back and get away from here?" he asked the woman. "And before you get deep into some killer strategy, we can't escape without replenishing our supplies. Not to mention our fuel."

"Those who have planned the appropriation of your little world should be doing just that right now," the woman said. "Replenishing your supplies. Your fuel generator will be modified such that a continuing supply can be distilled from available sources while you're in transit."

"Thanks," Don said, "but you'll forgive me if I tell you that sounds a little too good to be true."

The woman shrugged. "They think they're supplying the ship for themselves."

"Who's this *they?*" Don lowered his crossed leg and leaned forward, putting his elbows on his knees. Penny looked from him to the weapon and back again, but he refused to acknowledge her.

"A strain gone wrong," the woman said. "It happens from time to time. Good soldiers need a proper balance of autonomy and obedience. One of our strains has slipped over the line into disobedience and rebellion." She was looking at Don West now as if she were measuring him, Penny thought, and felt an abrupt wave of jealousy. "Oddly enough, I think you'd find them easier to get along with and understand. Under other circumstances, of course. And had you come into existence *here,* you would even be one of them, I have no doubt. But now your survival depends on stopping them."

Don took a breath, his face troubled. "OK, but first, what are we stopping them from doing? And why are *you* helping?"

"They want to take your little world, of course. Your 'ship.' They want to use it to prove there is a universe filled with other worlds where people can relocate to and live freely."

"Do they know where any of these worlds are?" Don asked.

"You have star charts in your onboard library, don't you?"

"Yeah, but there's nothing in this general vicinity that matches them."

"Then they'll simply use your hyperdrive."

"But without a receiving gate, they'll just — disappear."

"Like we did," Penny added.

"And that will be the end of our aspirations," the woman said. "Eventually, the story will become a myth that no one believes. And who knows if we'll ever develop a hyperdrive of our own. The people will continue as we always have — living through a designated time period, put to sleep at the end, remixed, reawakened —"

"Remixed?" Don's features went from curious to suspicious. "What do you mean, 'remixed'?"

"The formations are dismantled and the genetic material is remixed. It keeps damage to a minimum and prevents stagnation." The woman gave him a look. "What are you looking so alarmed at? I heard you all agreed to it yourselves when you came to the city. You would have gone ahead after the next cycle started —"

"Wait," Penny said. "Do you mean it's a thing where teams of people — crews or families — break up and get put to sleep? Or that you — you break the people themselves up into genetic material and . . ." she looked helplessly at Don.

"Genetic material is remixed," the woman said, impatience creeping into her voice. "If you know a way to do this without breaking people down into their components, please let me in on it."

There was a long silence.

"I'd tell you about sex," Don West said finally, "but I'm afraid of what you people would do with *that.*"

Chapter Eighteen

Maureen turned from the hologram of the schematic of the world to her husband. "I'd be shell-shocked all over again," she said with a small laugh, "but I think I'm starting to go numb. As if I really *had* finally seen it all and there's nothing more that can surprise me."

"I can remember you saying that when Penny got on the retro bandwagon and had her belly button pierced." John shook his head. "But I know what you mean. I'm starting to feel the same way."

"The longevity studies Judy was so wild about," Maureen said weakly. "She didn't realize that putting most of the population in hibernation was part of it." She paused, her stomach feeling tight and almost painful. "I wonder how long it would have taken either of us to catch on."

John shook his head. "We know now, thanks to the map Will found. And we'd better take advantage of it. Zoom in on that area around the *Jupiter Two* again so we can look at available routes."

"Or you could just tell this unit to show you the way," said the robot's twin almost conversationally. Maureen and John both jumped. *"This unit can determine with greater accuracy the route which*

gives you the greatest chance of arriving successfully at your little world."

"Fine. Good. Do it," John said, glancing at her worriedly. "Can you also do that without alerting anyone else?"

There was a pause. "If you wish," the duplicate said.

Maureen burst out laughing and then put her hand over her mouth. "Oh yes, *please.* If you don't mind."

John put both arms around her and held her tight.

"It's all right," she said after a moment, her laughter dying away. "I'm OK, really."

"You're sure?" he said, still holding on as he looked down at her.

"I'm sure."

"Good." He let go of her and headed for the door. "Because that's all the time we have for hysterics therapy. You can't get delirious again until we're safely away from here."

"Fine," she said, "but when the crunch is over, I'm having a nervous breakdown. I've earned it, I owe it to myself, and nothing is going to stop me."

John stopped her as she was about to step over the threshold. "Sorry, Dr. Robinson, *you* can't have a nervous breakdown. You're the mommy. It's not allowed. The best we can do for you is a conniption."

Maureen took his face in both hands and kissed him. "Thanks, I'll take it. It's the thought that counts."

The duplicate robot had rolled up behind Maureen and was waiting for her to go through so it could follow. *"It would be more efficient to dismantle your brain chemical and remix them in a way that would prevent the onset of a psychotic or semipsychotic episode."*

Maureen and John looked at each other. "I have a feeling I'm going to regret this," John said, "but explain that last statement."

All right, what is that creature going to do?

The question kept going through Judy's mind like a nagging rife from an annoying song. The alien seemed not to have moved so much as half a centimeter since she had been brought to the *Jupiter Two*. Didn't it understand?

Maybe it didn't. With her there, perhaps it thought that she was supervising everything that was going on. Or maybe it was catching up on its contemplation.

She turned from the sight of the creature to see her captors at work on the *Jupiter*'s food preparation system. They had taken the top and front paneling off and two of them were bent over working deep within the guts of the machine in a way that made her think of antique photos she'd seen of mechanics working on automobiles. Meanwhile, more of the parchment-colored, tattooed types had shown up and were poking around in *everything*. Half of them were running archived data on the navigation system while others were tracing every energy-delivery route from the pilot's console down to the engine room and back, using handheld devices shaped like squared-off, exaggerated barbells. These seemed to function as sensors on one end and a sort of electronic Swiss Army knife on the other.

Maybe I should ask them to open a bottle of wine for me, she thought a bit giddily. *I'd like to see an electronic corkscrew.*

She sat up abruptly. There *was* a bottle of wine aboard. More than one, in fact, and a corkscrew wasn't even necessary. In spite of all the weight and size restrictions placed on them, Maureen Robinson had foregone a few of her own belongings so she could smuggle a case of champagne aboard the *Jupiter Two.* Judy had discovered the champagne sometime after they escaped the destruction of the time-warped planet and gone to her mother about it, unaware that her mother was the culprit. Her mother, of all people — the original Mrs. Sobersides.

Her mother had made her swear not to reveal the secret of the bubbly cargo. *When we finally get to the planet, we'll be greeted by a work crew who will have seen nothing of their home for at least a decade. We can all celebrate the completion of the hypergate with a champagne toast, and maybe even have a bottle left to smash over a bulkhead and christen the thing properly.*

Someone poked her arm and she looked up to find the pale-green man standing over her. "Would you care to see how we have reconfigured your food production? Since we *will* be taking you with us for guidance —"

"No," she said, watching his hostile expression intensify. "Not until you all join me in a toast to the new venture."

"A toast?"

"A custom of my people, performed for the sake of placating our gods." She stood up. "If you expect to have any success at all, everyone must stop working, and carry out this action with us."

She held her breath while the green man thought it over. "All right," he said finally. "We're all just about done anyway."

Judy smiled. "I'll bring out the . . . uh — the sacrament," she said and hurried off to the subgalley that had served as an extra, minilaboratory for her mother. *Sacrament.* That was a good one. If Don West got wind of it, he'd never let her forget it.

When Don West got wind of it, she corrected herself, dragging the case of champagne out of the bottom cupboard at the end of the counter. "Sorry, Mom," she muttered, squatting to lift it the way Don West had showed her. (always from the legs, not from your back, thanks Don). "But it's an emergency. If they end up drinking it all," — she winced and hefted the box, balancing on one leg for a moment as she used her other knee to help readjust her grip on the box — "I'll mix up the very best bathtub gin replacement I can manage."

She made it out to the bridge and plumped the

case down on Don's chair just before she would have dropped it. Folding back the top flaps, she pulled out a bottle and held it up, examining the label. "Dom Perignon," she said approvingly, barely managing not to laugh at herself. As if she'd know the difference between Dom Perignon and Don Juan. *As opposed to Don Juan West, you mean?*

She shook the thought away and turned to face the green man. "It's all in order. Now go get Dr. Smith so we can begin."

"Dr. Smith is asleep," the green man said.

"Well, wake him up," she demanded. "Our gods are not easily placated when proper protocols are not followed."

The green man looked apprehensive now. The other two green people, along with the tattooed bunch, all looked at each other. Judy began to get a sinking feeling. "The sleeping cannot be awakened just like that."

She tried to ignore the foreboding creeping over her. "Look, he can't have been asleep for so long —"

"It doesn't matter. Once he's asleep, he's asleep." The green man frowned "Surely you understand that. He's been dismantled and because it's so close to the beginning of the next cycle, he'll sleep through that, and the next hiatus, before he can be remixed."

"Dismantled . . ." Judy swallowed. "I thought you meant like . . . dismantling the crew. Breaking it up because there was no more need for . . ." Her voice trailed off. "But it doesn't. Does it."

"Yes, the crew, dismantled. All. All of you, and all of you individually."

Amazing, Judy thought; your ears really did ring when your emotions were intense enough. *"Go get Dr. Smith right now,"* she ordered the green man, "or my gods will reduce you all to a little pile of cinders."

The green man sighed. "Dr. Smith is asleep. He will remain asleep until the beginning of the cycle after this one, when he will awaken within our people."

Judy grabbed the end of the console with one hand to try to stop shaking. "Are you telling me that it's already too late? That Dr. Smith has already been — he's been —"

No one spoke for a very long time. Judy stood shivering at the console, still holding the bottle of champagne. After awhile, some kind of activity resumed, but she wasn't sure what. Some kind of work going on around her father's console. The green man seemed to be waiting for something but she didn't at the moment care about anything.

Dear God, I'm sorry, she prayed silently, and it really was a prayer. *That poor, stupid wretch, that miserable, sad, lost soul, that doomed brute. Perhaps in the end, the guy never really had a chance. He was supposed to have been killed with us after he sabotaged the robot anyway, so maybe it was all borrowed time, from the moment we took off to when they 'dismantled' him a few minutes ago. Fate delayed but not denied. And maybe that's the case for us all.*

Ignoring the deep, painful hole that seemed to be opening up in her chest, she tore the foil off the top of the bottle and ordered the green man to get them some glasses to drink out of. Once those were distributed, she made them all line up and move past her holding out their glasses so she could fill them.

"We must — We must drink every bottle in this case," she said, wiping her eyes so roughly that she was practically slapping the tears off her cheeks. "Every bottle, do you understand?"

There was a murmur of assent.

"Because you have prematurely disposed of Dr. Smith, we have to make sure his share is drunk, or the gods will be . . . will be . . . be *very angry!*"

The green man started to say something.

"Shut up and drink!" she shouted at him.

He obeyed; they all did. Judy became aware that they were looking at her strangely and realized it was because she hadn't poured a glass for herself. There was one left on the console. She filled it and tossed it back as quickly as she could, refilling it again before she could think better of it.

Seeing as how they were susceptible to Smith's drug, they were no doubt equally susceptible to alcohol, Judy thought, choking down her third glass. Which meant that they would all be out of commission well before the case of champagne was finished. And that went double for her — Judy Robinson, M.D., D.V., Ph.D., and all-round tough cookie was, and always had been, the cheapest drunk on the staff of any institute, laboratory, or hospital.

On Earth as it is in heaven, and vice versa, she thought, unable to stop the tears now and no longer caring. It wouldn't be long before they were all so completely incapacitated that she could safely tumble to her quarters and give herself a shot of the drug her roommate at med school used to refer to as *instant sobriety*. Technically against the law, even now, but that was back on Earth, which was a long time ago and a galaxy —

"Don't go there," she muttered to herself, opening a third bottle.

Chapter Nineteen

Will and the robot watched as the two weirdos with the facial tattoos prepared a barrel.

They were hidden behind one of the people-laden "trees," far enough away that the weirdos wouldn't hear any small clicks or noises the robot might happen to make, or so Will fervently hoped. Lying on the ground next to the barrel was a very afflicted Zachary Smith. His skin looked almost gray and the whites of his eyes had gone completely red. At first, Will had been afraid the man was dead, but then he saw Smith shiver and spasm, as if his body were trying to be sick with nothing to draw on.

Tattoos Number 1 was pouring some kind of powder into the barrel while Tattoos Number 2 gave the barrel a shake every so often, as if to distribute the powder evenly. Then the first one bent down out of sight for a moment and came up with a hose. There was the sound of some liquid, too viscous to be water, sloshing into the barrel, and Will smelled something that reminded him of bread. Yeast? He frowned, biting his lip. Whatever it was, it was generating some serious chemical activity.

Tattoos Number 2 went over to Smith and started feeling his arms and legs, as if he were a piece of meat. "He'll go easily," Will heard the weirdo say. "It'll break him down in a matter of hours."

"Well, that's still not fast enough for this cycle," Tattoos Number 1 said, sounding a bit huffy.

"I never said it would be," Number 2 said, unruffled. "Frankly, waiting a cycle will do him good. Builds character. Extra time to absorb data as well as genetic material — who knows what he'll grow into."

"Or how many," added Number 1. "Definitely an enrichment for the pool."

"We can only hope. 'May the good strengths be fortified and the bad weaknesses diluted,' as the saying goes."

"It's been a long time since there was any new material added, hasn't it?" Number 1 moved over to Smith and pulled off his shoes.

"Ages. It's never happened in my lifetime," Number 2 said. "And I suppose I'm fairly old for a nonimmortal."

Will looked at the robot. "What are they talking about?" he whispered.

The robot was silent and Will realized that it couldn't speak softly enough without giving them away to the two weirdos.

"Project words," Will whispered. "Small size, use my hand as a screen." He held out his palm so they could both see. "And make it the short answer."

THE SHORT ANSWER: THEY ARE GOING TO DISSOLVE DR. SMITH INTO GENETIC RAW MATERIAL, WHICH WILL BE ADDED TO A

GENERAL POOL USED TO GROW NEW PEOPLE.

Will looked up at the heavy sacs overhead. "But — *what* new people?"

THE ONES YOU ARE LOOKING AT. NOT THIS TIME, BUT NEXT TIME.

"Next time?" Will stared at the words on his palm. "*What* next time?"

THE NEXT TIME ALL THE PEOPLE ARE DISSOLVED AND REGROWN. THIS IS WHAT THEY CALL HIBERNATION, SINCE NO GENETIC MATERIAL IS LOST.

Will's mouth dropped open. He looked over at the two weirdos, who had managed to strip Smith down to his underwear, an unremarkable pair of Jockeys and the kind of undershirt Don West wore to lift weights. "We've got to stop them," he said in a normal tone of voice, no longer caring if they heard him. "Robot, stop them! Save Dr. Smith!"

"Robot will save Dr. Smith." It obediently rolled toward the two weirdos, who had straightened up from Smith and were gaping in disbelief. To Will's surprise, they made no move to defend themselves or to run. *Wonder about it later!* he ordered himself.

"Robot — shock 'em!" he yelled. *"Stun, not kill! Repeat — stun,* not *kill!"*

"Stun, not kill," the robot repeated and sent a charge through weirdo Number 2, who was closer. Weirdo Number 1 watched open-mouthed as Number 2 jerked wildly and then collapsed.

"Both of them!" Will screamed desperately.

Weirdo Number 1 was turning to look at him when the robot let fly with another charge.

"Robot knew you meant both of them," it said as the first weirdo sank twitching to the floor and lay still. *"It can take a second to regulate the charge properly so that the organism isn't killed."*

Will paid no attention. He was squatting next to Smith, shaking him as hard as he could. "Come on, come *on!*" He straddled the man, took hold of the straps on his undershirt, and managed to pull him up to a sitting position. "Please, please, Dr. Smith. wake up, we have to go!"

Smith's head came up and his hideously bloodshot eyes opened. "Go? Don't be a fool, child. Nowhere to go. Lemme sleep." He tried to pull away and lie down again, but terror had given Will's strength a boost. He yanked Smith back up and forward, so that his face was nearly down on his knees.

Will looked over his shoulder. "Robot, help me! We've got to carry Dr. Smith to the *Jupiter Two*!"

The robot stretched out its arm as Will got around behind Smith, locked his arms around the man's torso, and tried to pull him to his feet. Dr. Smith wasn't resisting, but he really didn't have to — his all but dead weight defeated the boy's terrified strength. Will held on grimly, feeling the man starting to slide out of his grasp.

"Please, Dr. Smith," he said, almost sobbing.

"Please. Maybe there's nowhere to go, but if we get to the *Jupiter*, maybe we can hold them off —"

Smith's head came up again. "Not now. I need my vial." His head drooped forward.

"Dammit, Dr. Smith!" he hollered. He was about to say something else, but then an idea struck him. He lowered the pitch of his voice, trying to make it as deep and grown-up as possible "OK, *Smitty,* what do you say I pop your butt out the airlock?"

As an impersonation of Don West, it was only fair, but fair was good enough for the addled Smith. He got up off the floor immediately and stampeded right into the robot's outstretched arm, which bent him double. He went limp as the robot lifted him and Will sighed with relief.

Something, some bit of movement, caught his eye. At first he was afraid that another of the tattooed weirdos had come to see what was taking so long, or maybe to add someone else to the gene pool (*no, please, I won't think about that now, thank you*), but then he realized. He'd been looking up. One of the people in the sacs was moving. Just very slightly.

No, more than one. In fact, a lot of them. Will felt himself get queasy all over again.

"It is close to their time," the robot informed him helpfully.

"Great." Will forced himself to look away and start moving toward the area where the entrance to the *Jupiter Two* landing bay was supposed to be, according to the map. “Let’s get the hell out of here before they start falling like apples.”

At the sight of the bodies strewn all over the bridge, Don immediately went for his weapon. Then the smell of champagne hit his nostrils and he froze in puzzlement.

“Judy!” Penny ran for her sister, who was slumped in Don’s chair as if she were a rag doll someone had tossed aside after a particularly rough play session. Her hair was stringy and soaking wet, her face sweaty and flushed. Just before Penny would have reached her, she stopped short and screamed.

“No,” Don muttered to himself, going after the girl. “Please, no. Please —”

Then he stopped short as well and stared. Judy’s foot was resting on the back of a man’s pale-green neck. He was sprawled face down before her as if he’d been begging for something before being overcome.

The parchment-colored woman plucked a bottle of champagne out of the nearly empty case. “Is this an intoxicant?”

Don took the bottle from her. “A damned fine one.” He looked into the case; there was only one other left. “Where the *hell* did she get it?” He put the full bottle back in the carton with the other and bent down to pick up an empty one lying on the floor. “And, even better than that, *why?*”

“Because, Major, I couldn’t bring myself to *kill* them.”

He turned to see Judy standing unsteadily, leaning on Penny. Her eyes were red and puffy, as if she had been crying for hours.

"And I couldn't bring myself to *kill* them because I was crying too hard to aim a weapon." She nudged Penny, who supported her as she went over to Don, sparing a murderous look for the tattooed woman. "But I think I'm all cried out now. I think I might just be able to aim a weapon now. I think I might just be able to take care of a bunch of murdering, genocidal —" She made a clumsy lunge for Don's weapon and he caught her easily, pinning her arms behind her back again.

"Easy, Doc. She's on our side."

Judy struggled. "Oh, *sure.* That's what *they* tell you, the murdering scum. Do you *know* what they do? Do you *know?* They take people and they —"

"She told us, Judy," Penny said, putting a hand on her sister's shoulder.

"They *take* them — and they — they *kill* them! They *kill* them, and they, they, they —"

"Judy," Don said, *"we know."*

"They think they're still alive!" Judy wailed. "They think just because it's the same genetic material — they think it's the same people — only remixed somehow, remixed so that they're supposed to be even *better!* These people live the equivalent *of five years!*"

Penny started to interrupt but Don shook his head. "Let her get it out," he whispered.

"Except the ones we've seen! They take care of the city, they —" Judy sagged and Don let go of her wrists, putting his arms around her waist. "They just keep things going until the rest of the people grow back. I mean, they *think* they grow back. And then *those* people, the ones we saw, the ones we know, they'll all be killed. They'll all be killed." She turned to look at the tattooed woman "Except for *these.*" Don flinched; he'd never heard so much acid in her voice. *"These* are the *executioners.* They *call* themselves *caretakers,* and *they* tried to tell me that the people with all the colors, *they're* the immortal ones, practically immortal anyway. But *they,* the so-called *caretakers* —"

"They live out their lives looking after the city and growing new people."

Judy jumped in Don's arms and then struggled to run toward Maureen and John Robinson, who were standing in the entryway to the bridge. He let her go with a feeling of relief so intense that he felt his knees begin to shake.

A moment later, his relief vanished.

Will was still missing.

Chapter Twenty

"That word you keep using," the tattooed woman said. "The one that you use to describe us —"

" 'Murderers'?" Judy asked. She was calmer, but it was clear to Maureen that her daughter the ultracool, competent, level-headed doctor just could not detach enough from the situation to keep her loathing for these people from being obvious.

"That one. It doesn't translate." The woman tapped her ear. "Nor any of the others."

"What doesn't? You mean —" Judy thought for a moment. " 'Genocide'?"

The woman shook her head. "Untranslatable."

" 'Killers,' " Judy suggested " 'Executioners' 'Assassins.' "

" 'Terminators,' " Penny tried.

"Stop it!" Judy put a gentle hand over her sister's mouth. "This is horrible. You shouldn't even sit here and listen to it, let alone take part in it. Go to your room!"

Judy was still drunk, Maureen realized. In all the uproar, no one had thought to sober her up. She hurried to the lab for a disposable injector and came back in time to hear Judy ask, "How in the *hell* does a society that kills its people regularly *not* have a word for *death?*"

"Oh, 'ending.' " The tattooed woman nodded. "Only we caretakers experience *ending.*"

Judy spread her hands, looking from her father to Don West. "And they're the only ones who *aren't* killed. They get to live out a regular life span."

"If you can call being born an adult *regular,*" Penny added, a bit reproachfully.

Judy turned to look at her in surprise and Maureen chose that moment to give her the injection. The hairs-breadth needle sank into Judy's arm and vanished. She looked dizzy for a moment and then she shuddered. "Ew," she said, turning to Maureen with a grimace. "Thank you too much. If I'd been sober, I'd have told you I'd had too many emotional and psychological shocks and I should be allowed to sleep it off instead of going the instant route."

"Better luck next bender," Maureen said. "This caretaker says we now have enough of everything on board to keep us going for a long time. All we have to do is find Will and get out of here." There was a pause while her words seemed to hang in the air. "God. I just made it sound like — I don't know. Like one of those silly old-fashioned drama serials my grandmother was hooked on."

"What the hell." Don stood up and checked his weapon. "I'll go. I know where he is, or at least where he was."

"It's not necessary to go searching," the woman said. "A quick check of surveillance will give us his location." She took what looked like a blue handkerchief out of her pocket and spread it out on the console, smoothing it with one hand Maureen watched, amazed, as a schematic drawing appeared on the cloth.

"Say his name," the woman said to Maureen.

"William John Robinson. Will," she added. "Will Robinson."

A small circular point appeared on the cloth, became two points, and then three. The woman straightened up, looking wary.

"What is it?" Maureen asked tensely. "Where is he?"

"According to this," the woman said, "he's right outside."

Maureen started for the entryway but the woman caught her arm. "He's not alone."

"Who's with him?" John asked, drawing his weapon and activating it.

"It's not a who. Not a person."

"Must be the robot," Penny said, sounding relieved. "He goes nowhere without that robot."

The woman shook her head "The robot is clearly delineated. He has a — There's something alive . . . but *not* alive. But not inert. An energy —" She looked around at the unconscious bodies still lying mostly motionless on the bridge and then turned to Judy. "Do you know if any of these summoned more of them? Or summoned . . . something else?"

"Something else like *what?*" Judy asked.

"Anything, anyone," the woman said, exasperated. "Just tell me."

"No. I don't know. I don't think so but I can't say for sure."

Maureen swept past the woman before she could stop her again. "If my son is out there, I'm going to get him away from it, whatever it is."

"It could be another type of abomination," the woman called after her.

"Lady, I feel so poisonous right now that if I spat on the devil himself, he'd rot away on the spot."

She drew her weapon as she stepped into the darkness outside. The lights led away down the tunnel just as they had when they'd first arrived — when? How long ago had that been? A few days? Less than a week, she was pretty sure. Time here *was* weird.

There was a small noise behind her and she whirled, her weapon ready.

"I'm lucky you like me," John said, holding his hands up, his own weapon ready for use.

"Go back inside!" she whispered. "The *Jupiter* —"

"— has its pilot at the helm, ready to fly it out of here," he said. "No crew member goes out without backup, and Judy still can't pass a breathalyzer, so I'm elected." He paused. "You *do* like me, right?"

"Remind me to kiss and clobber you later," Maureen whispered. They crept around the side of the *Jupiter Two* together, John following her.

A moment later, she waved a desperate hand

at him, telling him to stay back and out of sight. Bracing herself, she moved forward, raising her weapon so that it was aimed upward.

"Hello, Will," she said.

"Hullo, Mom."

John Robinson held very still, just out of sight, and replayed the sound of his son's voice in his head. Something wrong, something strained in his voice.

"I'm glad to see you," he heard Maureen say in a carefully calm tone. "We thought you were lost. Both of you. All three of you, I mean."

"Mom?" Will said and made a small gagging noise.

"Don't!" Maureen said "Please! You don't have to hurt Will, don't you know that by now?"

John leaned back against the *Jupiter Two* and closed his eyes. *Smith.* It had to be.

"Spare me your maternal maunderings, madame," Smith sneered, but there was something wrong with his voice as well. It was thick and phlegmy, as if he were attempting to talk through a case of laryngitis and walking pneumonia. "I'm just trying to keep that tin-plated beast from shocking me."

"If I tell the robot to move away from you," Maureen said, "will you take your hand off Will's neck?"

There was no answer. John pressed his back against the smooth metal of the spacecraft, wishing there was something to hang onto so that he could keep himself from swinging into position behind Maureen and trying a shot at Smith's head.

"You can try," Smith said, "but there's only one thing I want, and I want it *right now.*"

"And you can have it, Zachary." Judy's amplified voice was somehow gentle. "Look up here, look at the windows. Can you see me?"

John wiped a hand over his face. God, but he wished *he* could see something.

"I don't know if you can see what I'm holding," Judy went on. "It's awfully small and hard to see from that distance. But it's what you want. What you think it is."

Someone — John hoped to hell it was Smith — made a tortured, suffering noise.

"Come and get it, Zachary," Judy said. "Come on. No one will harm you. No one will touch you. I've told them not to, they'll listen to me. I'm the doctor."

Smith let out a harsh cry. John heard him running for the entry to the *Jupiter Two* and he could stand it no longer. He stepped out to find Maureen kneeling next to Will, who was sitting up holding his throat. Tears were running down his face.

"I saved his stupid life," Will was saying, in between coughs. "I saved his stupid life and the minute he came to, he just went crazy, he says he doesn't want to leave, even though I told him —" Will cut off, looking from John to his mother and back again. "Oh, jeez, you guys aren't gonna *be-*

lieve what I found out about this place —"

"Try us," John said, putting an arm around his shoulders.

"Robot could shock Dr. Smith now," the robot informed them.

"It's not necessary anymore," Will said and coughed.

"*Maybe not for* you," the robot answered and rolled toward the *Jupiter Two.* John looked at Maureen in alarm and started to get up.

"Don't worry, Dad," Will said, catching his hand. "He's set on stun."

"I'd still like to know what that was all about," said John, helping his son to his feet.

Abruptly, Maureen drew her weapon again. "Get Will back to the *Jupiter,*" she said, adding, "don't argue!" when she saw that he was about to.

John bent down and whispered in his son's ear. *"Run. Now."* When Will disappeared around the side of the spacecraft, he drew his weapon and stood back to back with his wife.

"I thought I told you not to argue," she said.

"I didn't say a word," he told her, scanning the darkness for some kind of movement while he chastised himself for six kinds of idiot The tattooed woman had said there was something else out here, alive but not alive. While that might have seemed like a good description of Z. Smith, she hadn't been speaking in metaphors.

"I'd feel better if I knew you were in there to help Don and Judy in case Smith or those people —"

John felt her tense and he turned around.

"Well," he said, not raising his weapon so that it was pointed upward but keeping it trained in front of him. "I've been wondering when we'd meet you again."

The blue alien's expression was unreadable. It made no overtly threatening move, but its hands were out of sight behind its back and John didn't like that for a moment.

"Nothing to say now?" John prodded. "Nothing about getting us caught up with our contemplation? Too busy living in the skin and contemplating the nothing? Or has the entertainment in here been so gripping you haven't been able to tear yourself away from your surveillance monitors?"

Out of the corner of his eye, he saw Maureen take a quick look at him, her face pale and startled. How much more could she take, he wondered, before she collapsed?

For that matter, how much more could any of them take? How much more could *he* take himself?

As if his body had just been waiting for him to ask himself that question, he felt a wave of dizziness sweep through him in a very definite left-to-right path, as if the left side were tilting up while the right side was tilting down, and then vice versa.

God, please don't let me faint. Not now. If you let me stay on my feet now, I'll faint regularly for the next fifty years, but please —

"You are all completely unsuitable," the alien said finally.

"Good," said Maureen. "That's the best news I've heard lately."

"You will return the people you compromised."

Maureen and John looked at each other. "The people who tried to steal our ship, you mean," John said. "They're all yours. Our pleasure. Any other requests? Fries? Whipped cream? Artificial sweetener?"

"John." Maureen touched his arm, held on. "They tried to steal the ship so they could go on living."

A chill broke out on his neck and radiated across his shoulders, making him shudder. *Goose walked over my grave.*

"You're the real caretaker, aren't you?" Maureen said. "Or is there more than one of you?"

"We are sometimes more, sometimes fewer. This world was left to our care just as you have seen it — the city, the glowing ones, the place of regrowth, and all the cycles set. The people come together in the city for a set period of time. In that time, they must learn a certain number of things in a certain way. Then they are dismantled, remixed, and regrown. What they have learned is regrown with them so that in the next cycle, they can go on to learn other things."

"But —" Maureen let out a frustrated breath.

"The individual — you can't regrow the individual. They aren't the same people —"

"Of course not," said the alien smoothly. "They have learned. They are improved."

"No," Maureen insisted. "You don't understand. When you dismantle people, you —"

"Forget it," said John, putting his arm around her. "We're the ones who don't understand. And we'd better leave."

The alien made a sort of bow. "We would appreciate it. Perhaps the people could have learned from you, perhaps not. With your tissue informing theirs, an entirely new breed might have arisen in the next cycle. But we cannot risk losing tissue, and yours is a strain that apparently prefers to wander in the nothing confined to a small space for a limited period of life rather than enjoying the opportunity to live forever, and learn."

"There are other places, other worlds," John said. "It's not just *nothing* out there."

"But no place for people to live forever," said the alien.

"How long do *you* live?" Maureen asked, sounding suddenly fierce. "And who are you anyway? How do you fit into all of this?"

John didn't wait to see if the alien was going to answer or not. He took her arm firmly but gently and steered her back toward the *Jupiter Two.* She looked up at him questioningly.

"You heard it say that it, and its more or less fellow *things* were left in care of this world. So I suggest that we make a smooth and very hasty exit now, while we are invited to do so. Because I personally do *not* want to take even the slightest chance of running into whoever or whatever bolted this setup together in the first place. How about you?"

"Stop dragging your feet and let's *go.*"

Chapter Twenty-One

He woke with a start, which was the way he usually woke now, instead of oozing into a conscious state with a warm glow of pleasure, the sensation that, whether God was in his heaven or not, Zachary Smith certainly was.

But heaven was in the dead past, the very, very, *very* dead past, well out of his reach and beyond recovery.

Which made it doubly ironic that *recovery* was the word Judy insisted on using in terms of his treatment. *Rehab* he didn't mind; *recuperation* was tolerable (just). *Recovery* made him want to vomit.

In the beginning, he had thought he would never forgive Judy for strapping him into that chair, jacking it up to its full eight feet and leaving him there to twitch and scream and howl while they all somehow got rid of the bodies lying around. Not dead bodies, he learned later, just drunk ones. He would like to have heard *that* story, but no one would tell him. Not even Judy.

After that, everything faded in and out. By the time he'd seen his first day free of the physical addiction of the Kiss, they'd been in space for over a week. The world was long gone behind them; a careful poke around confirmed that the raw materials necessary for the Kiss had been removed, either destroyed or jettisoned.

Well, at least he wasn't going to suffer physically from deprivation any more. But God, the psychological addiction was . . . well, he had no words. For the first two weeks he'd spent free of the physical suffering, all he'd done was pace, either in his quarters or in the hallway outside, totally absorbed in *not* taking an eyedropper of the Kiss and putting it under his tongue, letting its warmth flow down into his body, seep into each nerve, bring new colors into his world and decorate his vision with patterns of lattices and Escher-like diamond shapes —

Don't go there, Zachary.

The voice in his mind was Judy's.

She had been there, not *every* moment, but every moment when he thought he might finally lose his grip and go completely mad, maybe even die of sheer *craving.* He would be pacing, pacing, pacing and suddenly think that he had to find some way to make the Kiss of Bliss again or run headfirst into the nearest wall to shut off the unbearable need in his mind.

And then somehow, there she'd be. As if she'd known exactly how far he could get on his own before someone had to intervene. And she must have known that she was the only one who *could* intervene.

You're thinking about how it was. I can tell. Don't go there, Zachary.

She bullied him through an exercise program; then she made him teach her rudimentary tourist

Portuguese, even though he'd protested that he hadn't spoken it in years. After awhile, he realized he was letting go of the addiction, the Kiss, and he understood that before, he hadn't wanted to because of the void it left.

The void was still there, but he could, now and then, plug it up, at least for awhile. Feeling better? Not quite the way to put it. Not feeling worse was more like it, and that was just going to have to do, until something better came along.

Someone laughed. Penny.

Smith sat up and swung his legs over the side of the bed. That was what had awakened him — Penny laughing. What time was it anyway? It felt like the damned middle of the night.

He put on his dressing gown, stepped into his slippers, and tried the door. It opened. Still not locked. Judy again — she'd convinced everyone else that keeping him locked up while he'd been hacking his habit would be cruel and unusual. They still watched him carefully, he knew that, but he wasn't quite as much a prisoner now as he had been.

But please, God, or whoever is in charge, I'm not a Robinson, either, all right?

He padded silently toward the bridge and then stopped. Penny and Judy were heads-together over one of the console screens, talking to each other in whispers and giggles. They were both in dressing gowns and pajamas as well, so he'd been right — it was the middle of the night, as reckoned by local *Jupiter Two* time. Pajama party, girls only; no boys allowed. He turned to go back to his quarters.

"Zach."

He turned around again. Judy and Penny were both looking at him with tentative smiles, though Judy's was somewhat warmer than her sister's. He put up a hand to indicate he didn't want anything.

"Wait." Judy got up and went to him, her eyes scanning his face in the highly professional doctor style he himself had once cultivated. "You look good. You're sleeping well."

"I'm comfortable," he said. Pause. "Thank you. Doctor."

"You're welcome. Doctor." Her smile widened and then she put a hand on his arm "Listen — after everything that's happened, I still wonder sometimes what I ought to believe. Or disbelieve. Sometimes when *I* wake up in the middle of the night, I think it was a fever dream or something. Sometimes I can even pretend that I really believe it was. But I know it wasn't. Isn't. And so forth and so on.

"But there is one thing I've always believed, and I find that I still believe it." She waited and he knew that was his cue to ask her to tell him what it was, but his voice didn't seem to be in working order. "It's this," she said finally. "All's well that ends well."

He took a breath and found his voice after all. "But, my dear Dr. Robinson, it hasn't ended."

"Don't go there, Zachary," she said.

Suddenly, she raised herself on tiptoe and kissed him.

It wasn't a passionate kiss, or even particularly substantial. Some might not even have called it a kiss at all, for it was just the softest feather-touch of her lips to his, and then she was hurrying back to Penny, who was wide-eyed and open-mouthed with a mixture of scandal, shock, and delight.

Smith stepped back, dazed, and got himself turned around to go back to his quarters. To his horror, Will Robinson was standing just behind him and, further down the hallway, Don West was leaning against the wall just outside of his room, arms folded, one foot bent up as if he were about to push off and launch himself at something. Or someone.

Instead, West simply reached down and opened the door, without otherwise moving a muscle.

"You've had a very nice time getting better, *Smitty,*" he said. "Now go back to bed. *Alone.*"

Smith drew himself up slightly. "I will if you will, Major."

In the Robinsons' quarters, Maureen rolled over and looked at John's face in the darkness. "Did you hear that?"

He sighed. "Yeah. I did. The long journey just got a whole lot longer. That's all we need."

Maureen was silent for a moment. "Maybe it is."

She felt him shift on the mattress beside her and throw one arm over her. "It is?"

"It's the most human kind of behavior in the world. It means we haven't given up, haven't lost our will to survive."

He moved closer to her. "You know, I think you're right."

Maureen laughed softly, taking him in her arms. "Yes, I can tell."

The employees of G.K. Hall hope you have enjoyed this Large Print book. All our Large Print titles are designed for easy reading, and all our books are made to last. Other G.K. Hall books are available at your library, through selected bookstores, or directly from us.

For information about titles, please call:

(800) 257-5157

To share your comments, please write:

Publisher
G.K. Hall & Co.
P.O. Box 159
Thorndike, ME 04986